Mine to Crave

Veteran K9 Team

Book 2

Kameron Claire

Snuggle Whore Press, LLC

Dedication

This series is dedicated to every individual
who signs a blank check on their ass
by enlisting in the Armed Forces
to serve their country—and to the
loved ones who support them back home.

We are Witty, Wicked & Wild wherever we go!

VETERAN
K9
TEAM

REPORTING
FOR DUTY

Chapter One
Kemp

I tense as soon as I see Vale's number on my phone. He's been a dick all day, but after what I said yesterday, I'm pretty sure I'm the asshole in this situation.

"Yeah?"

"Grab Linc and meet me at my house," Vale says without so much as a hello or go fuck yourself—either of which would have been acceptable.

"Why?" I slide my hand down my face and tug on my beard.

"We're going out. You're going to be my wingmen and hopefully entertain a cute little chick named Mari while I'm proclaiming my love for Cher."

I sigh. "Man, I can't tell if you had an amazing or horrible night last night. You were a dick today."

"I know, and I'm sorry, but that was partly your fault."

"I figured," I grumble.

"Call Linc, get dressed, slap on some cologne or

whatever fruity shit you wear, and be at my house in forty-five minutes."

"Alright. We'll see you in forty-five."

I hang up, dial Linc's number, put my phone on speaker, and push to my feet off my weight bench. Krieger, my four-year-old Shiloh Shepherd, lifts his head from his pillow in the corner to look at me.

"What's up?" Linc answers, the telltale sounds of Call of Duty or some other first-person shooter game blasting in the background.

"Get dressed. We're going out."

"Huh?" The video game mutes.

"Do I really have to repeat myself?"

Linc snorts. "Where are we going?"

I shrug, even though he can't see me. "Vale didn't say, but I'm thinking we're going to the Last Stand."

He sighs. "Is this about that chick he's been pining over for the last six months?"

Surprise has me glancing down at the screen. "You know about that?"

"Not really, but I've gleaned a few things from bits of conversations I've overheard."

"Yeah, well, we're his wingmen tonight and will be there to keep the girlfriends busy."

"Girlfriends? How many?"

Frustration laces through my words, making my bark a little harsher than I mean it to be. "I don't know, Linc! Could be one. Could be thirty. We won't know until we get there. Just worry about getting your sexy ass dressed and over to Vale's house in the next thirty minutes."

"Jeez, you're both grumpy old bastards for a couple of forty-year-olds."

"We're thirty-three and only six years older than you, asshat."

He chuckles. "Then act like it. See you soon."

"Yeah." I hang up and tug once again on my beard, inspecting my reflection in the mirror. He's not wrong. Some days I feel like I'm in my sixties even though I look like I'm built like a professional bodybuilder.

That's how I spend my time. Running operations at the VKC during the day and lifting to near exhaustion every night. Somewhere in there I eat, shower, play with Krieger and spend an embarrassing amount of time grooming my beard.

Occasionally, I play my guitar, but that's for me and only me.

I haven't dated in forever, and unlike Vale who got crushed by a cheating ex, or Janey who escaped an abusive asshole, or even Barron who had an amicable split from his wife because she no longer wanted to be a military spouse, I have no past heartbreak keeping me from the fairer sex.

Sure, I have childhood bullshit like everyone else, but my lack of desire to fall in love, get married, or have babies has no basis to be explored on a doctor's couch.

I'm a confirmed bachelor.

Always have been.

And I suppose, always will be.

Why don't I crave a relationship? The world may never know.

I climb the stairs from my basement home gym to the main level of my rancher. Like the other K9 trainers, I live on the east side of town. A couple of them, Linc and Barron, live in a newer development near the highway. Vale, Janey and I live in a community a couple of miles away that's thirty years old and in need of updating. Good bones, but removing the nineties golden oak cabinets and tan carpets is imperative.

It's on my list of things to do.

Janey moved here two years ago. Spring City was her home base before joining the Army, and it's where her grandfather left her the land on which she built the VKC. I followed almost immediately to help her out. No, there is nothing between us, although it's been questioned many times over the years. She's like a little sister to me—even though we are the same age—and I'd raze the earth to protect her. Some nasty shit went down with her ex that led to her separating from the Army early, and since my enlistment was up and I had nowhere else to go, I chose to move with her to Spring City.

To be honest, I felt the need to be close in case her mental state took a wrong turn.

I never should have doubted her. She's the strongest woman I know.

Instead, we formulated a plan, took the land and dilapidated buildings readily available on it, and started a business our K9 brethren could turn into their post-military home. We're well on our way, but the big changes come next year, once we find the right investors.

I always knew we'd get Vale here, although I wish I'd

been wrong. Nora was never right for him. She had a wandering eye while they were dating, always looking for an opportunity to trade up to someone with a higher status—because she is the kind of woman who wears her husband's rank as her own—but for some reason, she married him anyway. Vale, whom I've known since we went through boot camp together fourteen years ago, was content with being single until he met her. Janey and I have joked about her magical pussy, but in the end, who knows what makes one person fall head over heels for another?

I just know that with her, he did.

Now it seems he's fallen again.

I've already told him to slow his roll when it comes to this woman, and that got me a couple of days of attitude. I hate to see one of my best friends hurt, but then again, maybe he knows something I don't.

No risk, no reward and all that shit. Right?

Thirty minutes later, I'm showered, changed, and jumping into my Jeep to drive the few blocks between our houses. Linc pulls up and parks on the street at the same time I'm walking up to Vale's front door. We slap palms before I open the front door and walk into the house before announcing our presence.

Strijker greets us before I get a word out, his fur floating in the surrounding air. One thing about K9 trainers, we've accepted that our wardrobes will come with fur accents a long time ago.

"Hey, boy. Where's your dad?"

"Here." Vale walks in from the back bedroom, buckling his jeans with his boots unlaced. He looks from me to Linc and back to me. "I don't want to hear it. Just support me in this."

I raise my hands in surrender. "We're here. Are you ready to go?"

"Yeah." He grabs his wallet and keys.

"Where are we going?" Linc asks.

"Well, that's the problem." Vale sighs. "We'll start at the Last Stand, but we might need to hop around if she's not there."

"You don't know where she is?" Linc frowns.

"She's a little pissed at me right now." Vale looks pointedly in my direction and I cast my eyes to the ground.

Fuck, I guess I really did get into his head. "Sorry."

He sighs. "What's done is done. Let's just hope I'm not too late to fix it."

"Well, let's go. You want to drive separately, in case things go well?" I offer as positive energy to the situation.

He nods and we're off, all three of us driving to the Last Stand, a roadside country bar on the outskirts of town, halfway to the VKC where we all work. On the weekends, the Last Stand is a hopping place, doubling in size with a long dance floor perfect for two-stepping. They even put in a mechanical bull earlier this spring with an honest-to-goodness retired bull-riding champion running it. During the week, only the bar side is open, complete with pool tables, dart boards and a jukebox with every genre of music you can think of. That's the side we hang out on when the crowds aren't as crazy. The security guys let us bring our dogs in when we drop by on our way home from work.

I park my charcoal gray Jeep next to a cherry red Jeep with a six-inch lift and thirty-five-inch tires, dwarfing my stock Wrangler and reminding me of all the cool things I want to do to it.

"Good looking ride," Linc says, tilting his head in the vehicle's direction.

I nod. "Yeah. I wonder what crazy ass mud flinger owns it?"

We enter the bar as a unit and I watch as Vale's head immediately turns to the tables, his eyes and body intent on the two females playing a game. While I briefly catch the vision of a tall redhead, it's the short, curvy, dark-skinned beauty that captures my attention.

"Holy shit," I murmur under my breath. "She's beautiful."

If Vale hears me, he doesn't acknowledge the comment as he moves toward the table. "Can I play the winner?"

The redhead with the eight ball lined up in the corner pocket says dryly, "That would be me."

"I hoped that would be the case." He nods and turns to the shorty in the painted-on jeans and cleavage tugging mercilessly on her cotton tank top. "Mari, I assume?"

She smiles and I swear my heart stops. There's sugar and spice in those lips, the kind I'd love to taste. "Three hotties. Y'all are giving my reverse harem fantasies a starring lineup. Too bad at least one of you isn't available."

Vale gestures to me. "These are my buddies, Kemp

and Linc. Kemp's buying the next round. Can you help him order the right drinks?"

I plaster on a smile as I offer her my arm. "This way, milady."

Mari hands Vale her pool cue and lowers her voice, saying something to him before turning her hazel eyes framed by thick dark lashes to me. With a coy smile, she slips her arm into mine. "Lead the way, handsome."

She, Linc, and I walk up to the bar where our normal bartenders, Tess and Dawn, are busy restocking liquor bottles and performing inventory. Tess turns to us with a smile. "What can I get you?"

I tilt my head to Mari. "Tell the lady what we'll have."

Her smile grows wider as she rattles off a well-practiced order. "Ten shots of Jameson and five Bud Lights."

Pressing my lips together, I exchange a look with Linc and nod appreciatively in her direction. "You don't mess around."

"I really don't." She turns around, looks me up and down, then Linc, and then back to me. "Are you the one shit-talking my girl?"

Oh, damn. So it's going to be like that. "Not her specifically."

"What's the matter, Gandalf? You don't believe in love at first sight?"

"Gandalf?" I instinctively stroke my beard, which causes her to laugh.

"Don't worry. I think Gandalf is sexy. Besides, I'm

trying to come up with a good nickname for you, so it may not stick."

Internally, I'm debating how much I hate being called Gandalf. I shake my head and get back to the topic at hand. "It's not that I don't believe in love at first sight, but I don't want to see my friend get hurt again."

Tess sets down a tray of Jameson shots and gives us an iced bucket of beer. "Whose tab is this on?"

I pull out my credit card and hand it to her. "That would be me."

Mari hands me and Linc a shot and then tilts her head in Vale and Cher's direction, their foreheads nearly touching in close conversation. "I don't want to see my best friend hurt either, but I don't think we can stop what's going on between them."

"Nor do I want to," I say as Vale slides his hands over Cher's ass and pulls her flush against his body. He claims her in a not-safe-for-public-consumption kiss—not that anyone else is here to see it.

Mari giggles, and I clear my throat. "Dude."

Linc lifts his glass and says loud enough for everyone to hear. "To the happy couple."

We toss back our shots and double-tap our empty glasses on the bar. Mari hands both Linc and me a beer, and we lean back against the bar, an awkward silence descending between us.

"So..." Linc grabs Mari's attention with his charm-your-pants-off smile. I don't know why, but it instantly grates on me. "What exactly is a reverse harem?"

Mari chuckles and picks at the label on her bottle. "A

reverse harem is when one woman has the sexual attention of three men—at the same time."

He frowns and looks at me. "How would that work?"

I shake my head and groan. "Dude, don't ask that."

She giggles. "Well, according to the books I've read, very creatively."

"Books, huh?" He smirks and I feel like he's flirting.

Oh fuck no, he's not coming on to her.

"Shut up." I throw him a pointed look.

She giggles again. "I'm wild, but I'm not that wild."

"How wild are you?" Linc raises his brow, ignoring my veiled warning and not backing down one bit. I swear to god, I'm going to kill him—which is crazy. I have no claim over this woman and I suck at flirting, but he's doing exactly what we were brought here to do.

Distract her.

She grins sheepishly and dips her head, but says nothing.

Linc's eyes slide my way, and he gives me an almost imperceptible nod in her direction. If he's asking if I'm interested, the answer is yes, even though that means absolutely nothing.

I don't flirt.

I don't tease.

I don't pursue.

Not because I'm too good for it, but because it feels awkward.

"What about you two?" Mari grabs a second round of shots and passes them to us. She lifts, shoots it down and double taps the glass. "Are either of you wild?"

"What do you consider wild?" I raise my brow, setting my empty shot glass next to hers.

"Oh... whips, chains, leather masks, ball gags, ten people in a room wearing college mascot heads and jockstraps."

"Which mascot head would you choose?" I ask with genuine curiosity, utterly ignoring the rest of her comment—for now. I'm not into the whips or chains, but restraints are a different conversation.

"Hmmm. I'd have to think about that. Who's your team?"

Oh, damn. Is she flirting with me over Linc—the VKC's chick magnet?

Impossible. "I'm not sure."

"Mmmm. Well, you think about it and let me know, and I'll see what I can do." Mari tilts her head, her eyes glued to my face. "I desperately want to stroke your beard. Do you get that request a lot?"

I shrug. "Not a lot."

"You know what they say," Linc interjects. "You touch his beard, and he gets to touch your butt."

"I'd be okay with that." She smiles up at me.

Linc shakes his head. "I think we've fulfilled our task this evening. If you don't mind, I'm going to head back to my pizza and game at home."

Panic wars with relief in my chest.

He isn't going to pursue her—that's good.

He's leaving her alone with me—not as good.

The only women I get, however short or long that might be, is because they want me. Like I said, I'm awkward and constantly sticking my foot in my mouth like I did with Vale two days ago. I'm not malicious, but somehow I always pick at an insecurity that I didn't know was there.

"Fine with me, man. Are you good to drive?"

"Yeah." He offers his hand to Mari. "Nice to meet you. Take it easy on the big guy."

She chuckles. "I make no promises."

He nods with a knowing smirk on his face. "See you tomorrow."

"Yeah." I watch him walk out and then glance in Vale and Cher's direction—the two of them making out like a couple of teenagers—before turning my attention back to Mari, who looks up at me with genuine interest. Something about her unsettles my stomach and I don't think it's the two shots of Jameson.

Should I ask her out or forego entanglement considering she's Cher's best friend? If things don't go well between Vale and Cher, the last thing I want is to add complications by having any attachments, no matter how fleeting, to her best friend. I'm not the smoothest motherfucker and if we hooked up casually once, twice, or even a dozen times, eventually it will end, but we'd still have to see each other if Vale and Cher stayed strong.

Besides, considering my mouth, it's just a matter of time before I offend this cute shorty standing in front of me. And then what?

VETERAN
K9
TEAM
REPORTING
FOR DUTY

Chapter Two
Mari

Damn, I thought Vale was a hottie the night Cher met him six months ago, but his friends make him seem almost average. Are all K9 trainers this hot? We had two with us on this last deployment, but I wasn't overly impressed by either.

Weird.

Linc is a good-looking guy—there is no denying that—but he's a little too pretty for me.

I like my men rough but groomed.

Strong but gentle.

Hard but soft.

I like men who look like Kemp, except he's the next version of who I normally go for. First, let's talk about his biceps, which I swear are thicker than my thighs—and I have a gloriously juicy booty to be proud of. His chest is wide and pulls his shirt tight to hint at all that lickable muscle, and I doubt he skips leg day. He's got a thick neck covered by a perfectly trimmed beard that looks so soft. I can imagine straddling his lap with his arms around my waist while I comb and braid his beard.

I wonder if he'd let me do that?

His auburn hair is a little long on top, but they shaved the sides close, which gives him an overall Viking vibe. Maybe instead of Gandalf, I'll call him Ragnar. He's got blue eyes, so there's a good chance he's got some Nordic ancestry rushing through his veins, anyway.

I've always wanted my very own Viking, not that I'll keep him for long. I'm not so great with relationships.

Date casually? Sure.

Commit to someone with an expectation that they will truly commit to me in return? No way.

I know better, and I'm not stupid enough to believe that one man will settle for one woman. They never have in my experience.

My father, uncles, cousins, most of my friend's husbands and all my high school boyfriends—cheaters.

No man is satisfied with one woman, so why should I put my heart on the line to learn the same lesson every woman in my life has learned before me?

I love Cher like a sister and I want to warn her away from Vale, but maybe she'll be one of the lucky ones who meets a good man not looking to stroke his ego with the pussy of the month.

Yeah, I got that term from my auntie.

And if Vale isn't a good guy, then I'll be there to key his truck and slash his tires before bringing her a bottle of tequila and a pint of ice cream—not to be ingested together.

Barf city.

Back to my Viking.

"Alone at last." I bat my eyelashes in his direction.

"Were you wanting to get me alone?" Kemp raises his brow with his beer raised halfway to his lips.

I shrug. "Linc's hot, but you are so much more my type."

"Am I?" He seems genuinely surprised.

I snort. "Yeah. What woman doesn't want a tall, broad, beautiful lumbersnack of her own?"

"No more Gandalf, huh?"

"I'm thinking you are more of a Ragnar."

He smiles, white teeth flashing behind his thick hair. "Viking lore. Now you're speaking my language."

"Because of the show?"

"That and the History Channel. I watch a lot of stuff like that."

"So you're a geek on top of an expert K9 trainer and muscle-bound hottie?"

A blush hits the tops of his cheeks, and it's so damn cute, I want to see more. "I guess."

"So, what's your type, Kemp?" With all the hints I'm laying down, he better say me. I mean, I'm practically giving it to him.

The line and tasty worm is in the water, buddy.

All you have to do is bite.

"I like assertive women. I need a woman who will smack me upside the head."

"I'd be happy to smack you around if that's what

you're into." I grin and turn my attention to Cher and Vale, who walk up to us hand in hand.

"We're taking off," Vale says without preamble.

"Hopefully, you two can behave yourselves without adult supervision." Cher arches a knowing brow in my direction.

"What fun would that be?" I clap back.

"Do you want your shots?" Kemp motions to the untouched drinks on the bar.

"Not tonight." Vale shakes his head. "You enjoy them. Thanks for buying."

"Happy to support, brother." Kemp clamps his big hand on Vale's not small shoulder, the two of them speaking volumes without saying a word.

My god, these guys are massive—although I'm not coming from the best frame of reference at five-foot-three and a half.

Yes, the half-inch is important.

"I'll call you tomorrow." Cher looks from me to Kemp and back to me—twenty years of friendship having our own conversation without saying a word.

"Sounds good. I'm glad you two worked it out." I smile, truly happy for my friend. The things she told me about Vale while we were deployed—well, let's just say he wouldn't make eye contact with me if he knew the blow-by-blow report I'd heard.

I hope he's a good guy.

I really, really do.

After they exit the building, Kemp clears his throat. "Are you calling it a night?"

"Why? Are you offering to take me home?" I smirk and grab two of the remaining shots, offering him one.

He tosses it back with ease and pins me with an intense eye. "I can't tell if you're kidding or not."

I chuckle, grab the last two shots, and sashay my fine ass to the jukebox. "Bring the beer bucket, babe."

He follows and sets them down on a tall table, taking a seat on the barstool. He's contemplative, with his eyes glued to me. There's something about the way he watches me, intense, but not leering—like a highly trained dog waiting for the signal to pounce. Nothing about having his eyes on me creeps me out, but maybe that's because I want his attention on me.

And I want him to pounce.

I mean, he is the sexiest beast I've had the pleasure of talking to in a long time.

"Do you like music?" I walk up to the jukebox and bring up the menu.

"I do."

"Any genre in particular?"

"Anything with a guitar riff."

I glance over my shoulder at him. "Do you play?"

His eyes cast down, and he nods reluctantly. "I tinker."

I arch my brow. "Will you play for me?"

"Probably not," he says flatly.

"Why not?" I jut my bottom lip.

"I don't play for other people."

I turn back to the jukebox and select a couple of rock songs. My musical taste is as wide and varied as my fashion sense. I love it all and move my body to hip hop and club music as easily as I can rock out to country and alternative. I start tonight's playlist with "Whole Lotta Love" by Led Zeppelin. The guitar intro alone is enough to keep this conversation going.

"What if I danced for you?" I swing my hips and lift my arms over my head, flashing him a teasing smile. "Would you play for me?"

Kemp's eyes darken, and his chest expands with the deep breath he takes. "Are you always such a flirt?"

"Yes." I grab one of the two remaining beers out of the bucket and take a sip, my hip brushing against his knee. "But don't assume you aren't special."

He grabs the other bottle, holding on to it with both hands which rest between his splayed knees. "How am I special?"

"Well, when I heard about you, I had decided that if we ever met, I was going to take a bite out of your ass for making your boy doubt his feelings for my girl. But now that we're here, I want to take a bite out of you for other reasons."

"Back to our conversation about being wild." He smirks.

"If you want to know how wild I am, take me home with you." I step forward, pushing my hips between his knees, and wiggle my ass. "You know you want to."

"Yeah, I do." He sets his beer down. "But there's one huge problem."

"What's that?"

"If things between Vale and Cher are nearly as

serious as I believe he intends them to be, and you and I don't work out, it'll make our friendships awkward." He places his hands on the outside of his thighs, purposefully not on me—which only makes me want him to touch me more.

"Who's asking for a relationship, Ragnar?" I step forward and set my beer down before laying my palms flat on his massive pecs, my fingertips stroking the ends of his beard. Damn, it is soft. "I'm talking about having a little fun, and that's it. I just got back from a six-month deployment and could use a good time. Couldn't you?"

"No expectations?" He lifts one brow. "Pure pleasure?"

I shrug my shoulders and look up at him through my lashes. "If you're up for the job."

He takes another deep breath and shifts his hips, pushing his knees farther apart. "I've been up for the job since we walked in and I saw you in those painted-on jeans and hiking boots."

That comment has me looking down at the bulge in his pants. "Oh. Does that mean you're ready to go?"

"Ready when you are." He finally, FINALLY, moves his hands to my hips and lowers his head.

I tilt my head back and lick my lips, the fire in his eyes igniting with the simple action. "Maybe you want a taste first?"

"You willing to kiss me in public, Shorty?"

"There's no one watching us, Ragnar."

He nods but says nothing. Tightening his grip, he guides me back and stands but doesn't claim my mouth like I'm hoping. "I'll close out my tab, and then we can go."

Hmmm. That was quite the mood shift. I wonder what I said?

I decide to forgo the last two shots and the rest of my beer, considering I need to drive to his place. Although I feel fine and can hold my liquor well, I am cognizant of the fact that I'm short, and three shots against one hundred and fifty pounds is pushing up against the legal limit.

Kemp comes back and nods his head to the untouched liquor. "I'm glad you didn't feel the need to finish those."

"Why is that?"

"Now I don't have to wonder if it's you or the Jameson talking." He offers me his hand and we walk toward the door.

"This is all me, handsome."

"Good. Let's go."

I wave over my head at Tess and Dawn, who both stop what they are doing to fan their faces and toss me a couple of thumbs up.

Yeah, I come here more often than Cher and have gotten to know the female bartenders and their boyfriends. One boyfriend I like, the other I despise—pretty sure he's a big-time cheater—but I'm not close enough to either woman to say anything without proof.

"Where are you parked?" Kemp looks around the mostly empty parking lot.

"Right here." I point to my red beast which is parked next to a charcoal gray stock version of my precious Jeep.

"This is yours?" His jaw drops. "I was checking her out when I arrived. Nice lift. How do you climb your short ass into this giant?"

I turn into his chest and slide my fingertips into his waistband. "The same way I'm going to climb you—with authority."

He slides his hand around my waist and down my ass, lifting me as if I weigh nothing. I throw my arms around his neck, our lips finally within kissing distance. Kemp takes a step forward and places me on my seat since my Jeep doors and hardtop are currently off. Before he can take a step back, I lock my ankles behind his back and hold him in place. "You touched my butt. Now I get to touch your beard."

"As soon as I get you home, you'll be riding my beard."

Okay... flirty fun is over.

I'm now in full-on fountain-waiting-to-erupt mode. "What are we waiting for?"

Kemp leans forward until I'm arching back and kisses me softly, holding his lips to mine without pushing for more. It's tender, but strong, as if to make my body a promise I expect him to keep.

I melt a little and unlock my ankles. "Following you, big boy."

"This is me." He points to the Jeep parked next to me. I live a couple of miles away, not too far from Vale and Cher.

"I'll be on your ass the entire way."

We drive a few miles and sure enough, he lives a couple blocks away from Cher—which means he only lives a couple blocks from me with one major roadway separating our neighborhoods. I pull into the driveway behind him, comforted by the fact that he isn't worried about someone seeing my car parked in front of his place late at night.

There will be no jealous girlfriends or the like disrupting our evening fun.

"I hope you're not afraid of big dogs." He waits for me to join him before sliding his key into the front door.

"I'm not."

Kemp swings the door open and a big Shepherd is waiting for us, eerily quiet as he looks me over from his seated position.

"*Hier*," Kemp says and the dog stands and comes to his side, his head up and eyes locked on his trainer. "Do you want to pet him?"

"Of course." I'm used to playing with Sookie—Cher's Husky-Malamute—who is kind of a big goof.

But a highly trained military K9? No.

"Why don't you take a seat on the couch so he doesn't knock you over? He's going to want to nuzzle you. I can tell."

I take a seat and he releases his dog, who comes right to me and rests his furry face on my lap. "What's your name, beautiful?"

"Krieger."

"What does that mean?" I rub my thumbs in circles

over his snout and around his eyes. The big dog leans into me, his tongue lolling out of his mouth.

"It kind of means war in German. Most of our dogs have names that mean warrior, soldier, god or the devil in one language or another."

"Is this a macho testosterone thing?" I giggle and flash him a teasing smile.

"No. Janey's first dog was Gwar and her current dog is Macha. It's hard to deploy with a team of badass Army Rangers and command Fluffy to do a perimeter check."

"Awww, but how great would it have been to cheer Fluffy on while she tears someone's ass up?"

He tilts his head and chuckles. "Good point."

"Think I could use your bathroom and freshen up?" I push to my feet, much to Krieger's dismay.

"Sure." He nods and points down the hall of his rancher. "First door on the left."

I trail my fingers over his taut stomach as I pass by and swish my hips seductively, just in case he needs a reminder why I'm here and what we should be doing.

Most guys would already have me naked, bypassing the puppy introduction or gentlemanly hospitality and dragging me into their bedroom.

Is Kemp's slow roll a sign that he's changed his mind?

Or is this about his need for an assertive woman?

I can be assertive.

Who am I kidding? I'm always assertive, much to my dismay. The men I date, I never truly relax with, which means I never let my guard down or give up control. Part of me would love to do so, but that requires trust—something I don't give easily.

In the bathroom, I check my hair and freshen up my lip gloss. We've only been home a few days, and I spent all day yesterday getting twists put in, so I know my hair is on point. I hoist the girls up and pull the top of my tank down, just to make sure my cleavage is as drool-worthy as possible. If he's changed his mind, it isn't because I don't look amazing.

Don't get me wrong; I have my insecurities like all women, but how I look isn't one of them. I love my curves and know how to use them. While I'm a little heavy for regular Army, the reserves are a bit more relaxed, so they don't bother me about it. I can pass my PT tests with no problem and I'm very active, so they let the weight on the scale slide a little.

If we want to pick at my insecurities, we'll have to deep dive into my inability to love or accept love.

But I have no time for that tonight.

Walking out of the bathroom, I notice the living room lights are down, but the lights over the breakfast bar are up and there are two cold beers poured and waiting for us. Beyond the kitchen, I see through the window that Kemp is in the backyard with Krieger, but then they walk out of sight and the Shepherd comes running into the house from the back bedroom.

I guess he has a door from his bedroom to the backyard. Cool.

My Viking walks in a minute later, his boots off and T-shirt untucked. "Is the beer okay?"

I nod and take a sip. "Perfect."

He walks up behind me—the back of my head hitting him chest high—and reaches over me for his mug. I lean back, tilt my head up, and bat my lashes while sliding my palm up his hard thigh. Kemp bends down and puts his mouth between my shoulder and my neck, kissing me lightly and inhaling deeply. "You smell good."

Grinning, I put my beer down and spin to face him, tilting my chin up high. "I taste good too."

That's all the invitation he needs to remove the space between us, sealing his mouth over mine. He picks me up, and once again I wrap my legs around his waist while slipping my tongue between his parted lips. The man tastes like peppermint and I think he swished some mouthwash before coming out of his bedroom.

How thoughtful. If we were at my house, I would have done the same.

No matter, it won't take long for us to taste like each other because I have every intention of running my tongue over every inch of this man.

Kemp grows more assertive by the second, pulling me tighter against his body as our tongues slip and slide in an erotic dance.

"Fuck, you are sexy." He pants while his fingers flex against my thighs. "I like the way you feel in my hands."

"And I'm betting I'll like the way you feel in my mouth. So take me to your bedroom, where we can get naked and find out."

VETERAN
K9
TEAM
REPORTING
FOR DUTY

Chapter Three
Kemp

Because of my size, I decided a long time ago that I would let women lead our intimate encounters. The last thing I want to do is make somebody feel unsafe, so I've grown accustomed to appreciating women who know what they want—especially when it's me—and letting things progress from there.

If I was more outgoing, I'd wear my desires on my sleeve and let a woman know that not only am I interested but also tell her all the things I want to do to her—some of which fall outside the spectrum of vanilla sex. Unfortunately, because I'm not immersed in an alternate lifestyle or the kink community, I have no idea how to express my desires or connect with a woman who might also be down for the things I'm interested in exploring.

It's a delicate exchange, and considering I don't form long-term relationships, the trust required to have these conversations never gets established.

In many ways, Mari is about fucking perfect. I don't

think I've ever met a woman more sure of herself in my life and it makes me wonder if she's like this in everything.

Her job?

Her faith?

Her future?

I can't think about that right now. Not while I'm laying her down on my bed and unlacing her Treks. "These are good hiking boots. Do you climb mountains often?"

"Not since I've been back, but last fall I tried to get out at least once a weekend." She unbuttons her pants and frantically wiggles them off her hips at the same time that I grab them from her ankles and slide them down her smooth legs.

Mari sits up and pulls off her tank top before playfully flinging it at my face.

I chuckle, pressing my hand flat against her sternum and pushing her gently to her back before she can unhook her bra. "Relax, beautiful. We've got all night. I know we said there are no expectations, and that this is pure pleasure, but that doesn't mean we have to rush."

Her brow furrows, but she says nothing as I glide my fingertips softly over her skin. Tracing the edges of her lace-lined bra with a gentle touch, her flesh prickles into goosebumps and her nipples pebble into firm peaks as her breaths become more shallow. She watches me intently as I flick open the clasp on her bra and peel back the cup, lowering my head and sucking the pert bud into my mouth.

Mari reacts superbly, moaning softly and arching her back.

Biting down, I alternate between sucking and nibbling, testing how much pain she likes and how much is too much. She threads her fingers into my hair, pulling me close and then clenching her fist to back me off without uttering a word.

Perfect response for a man of few words.

I move down her body and press my face against her cotton-covered pussy, biting playfully through the thin fabric. "You ready to ride my beard, Mari?"

"I thought you'd never ask."

I slide her panties down and spread her thighs to take my first taste. She's gloriously wet and I groan low in my throat as her sweet arousal coats my tongue. Her clit is plump and sensitive to the touch, which tells me she'll explode once she gets her rhythm.

Sliding my hands under her ass, I roll onto my back and pull her with me. She giggles as she adjusts, her ass perched on my chest. "You really want me to ride your face, huh?"

"Did I stutter?"

"I've got thick thighs."

"I'll tap out if I have to, but I wouldn't count on it." I smack her ass. "I'd rather suffocate than admit weakness. Now get your beautiful ass up here."

I guide her to where I want her and wrap my hands around her waist, pulling her down and running my tongue from her cunt to her clit before sucking the plump bud between my lips. The harder I flick and suck the bundle of nerves, the harder Mari grinds her pussy down, rubbing her lower lips across my beard and moaning her appreciation of the delicious friction. "Oh fuck, that feels good."

Cupping her breasts, I tease her nipples while alternating between thrusting my tongue inside her and rubbing my beard across her clit until her knees tighten around my head and she bears down on my face. "Oh fuck, oh fuck, oh fuck."

Cum rushes out of her as her orgasm takes over, flooding my mouth and coating my whiskers. I gulp down every drop, her arousal sweet nectar, her cunt my honeypot. It's a taste I could become addicted to, which is a dangerous thought for me to have.

She falls limply off of me, her breaths coming in desperate pants. "Oh, Ragnar. I really like your beard."

"Just my beard?"

"Your mouth, teeth and tongue are pretty extraordinary too."

Chuckling, I sit up, pull my T-shirt off, and wipe my face before throwing it to the floor. I look down at her, once again tracing my fingertips gently over her skin. "I think you're extraordinary."

She lifts on her knees and raises her brow. "Don't give me credit yet. Let me earn your praise."

Pushing me down, she slides her hands down my chest and over my abs to work the buttons on my fly. "You have a magnificent body, Kemp. Do you compete?"

"No." I hiss as she rubs her palm over my erection, my mind struggling to form words.

"Why not?"

"I'm not into showing off my body." Or my scarred back and face, but I leave that comment unsaid. She hasn't asked about it yet, and if she's disgusted by the deep lines a roadside bomb gifted me nearly ten years ago, she doesn't show it. "I work out in my basement versus going to a gym most days."

She leans down and presses her lips to my sternum, using her tongue to trace the ridges in my abdomen. "All this work and you don't show it off? Who have you been saving it for? Me?"

I groan softly in response as she grips my cock, pulling my erection free from the confines of my jeans, her thumb swiping over the pre-cum spilling out of the tip.

"Oh damn." Mari brings her eyes up to me. "You're magnificent everywhere."

"Glad you approve." I arch my brow and look down my body at her, dark thoughts running through my head. What I wouldn't give to put her on her knees with a pretty rope lacing her arms behind her back while I feed her every inch until she's choking with mascara-streaked tears running down her cheeks.

The vision comes unbidden and I shake my head, reminding myself to focus on the here and now. I have a gorgeous spitfire in my bed, lowering her head to take me in her mouth.

I need to enjoy her however she comes... and as often as she comes.

Mari keeps her eyes on mine as she runs her tongue

from my balls to the tip, swirling teasing circles around the swollen head. I take a deep breath—the desire to cup the back of her head and fuck her plump lips so tempting and so forbidden. Flexing my hands and gripping my sheets, my hips involuntarily buck as she takes me deep into her hot, wet mouth and works me until I'm on the brink of eruption.

I can't stop myself from pulling her off my cock and dragging her up my body to claim her mouth in a punishing kiss. Reaching over to my bedside table, I retrieve a condom while unceremoniously kicking off my jeans. It takes seconds to sheath myself and grip her hips —not nearly enough time to slow myself down—before I'm slamming home inside her hot, wet depths.

We groan in unison, neither of us moving as I will my impending orgasm back and her pussy adjusts to my size, her inner walls pulsating and keeping me on the edge.

"Oh wow, big guy." Mari brings her dark eyes down to me.

"Don't move." I flex my hands on her hips, wondering if I'll bruise her at all. If I am too rough, she doesn't seem to mind.

"Gotcha worked up, eh?" She flashes a taunting grin —half playful, half challenging.

"You have a wicked mouth, Mari."

"Mmmm. That's some excellent praise for my oral skills."

I nod, guiding her hips into a slow roll that makes the head of my cock graze against her spongy G-spot. Mari's eyes roll back and she moans softly, dropping her head forward and grinding her clit down. I slip my middle finger between us, giving her that rough spot she desperately craves as my release threatens to spill over.

Not yet, man. Not yet.

Sliding my free hand up her side and over her full breast, I cup her neck and pull her lips down to mine, plunging my tongue into her mouth. Mari melts against me, kissing me with the passion I crave, yet somehow always escapes me. It doesn't take long before she's jerking her hips, taking over the slow grind I've established to chase her release.

"Oh fuck. Oh fuck, oh fuck, oh fuck!" She presses her forehead into my neck as her cunt clamps down around my cock and pushes me over the precipice I've been carefully balanced on for the last several minutes. As her pussy pulsates, I take control from underneath, pumping up into her to drain my balls of every drop.

She collapses on me in a heap, the two of us panting in silence as we attempt to catch our breath. "Wow, Ragnar. You rock."

"Same, Shorty." I chuckle and smooth my hand down her back.

Mari rolls off me and lands on my side, her eyes glued to the ceiling fan above us. An awkward silence descends as our breathing calms and I—a man notably of few words —am infused with a desperate need to fill it.

"You wore me out, woman."

She chuckles softly. "It was a good ride."

"Give me a few minutes and we'll go again."

"Really?" She finally brings her eyes to mine, a firmly raised brow challenging me on some unspoken level.

"Ten, maybe fifteen minutes." I shrug, sitting up with my hand wrapped around my cock to hold the condom in place. "Let me clean up and we can discuss what kind of breakfast I can make you in the morning."

Mari sucks her breath in when I turn my back to her and I realize that she's finally seeing my scars for the first time. They aren't extensive—I fared much better than most after several deployments to hostile territories—but they aren't pretty to look at either.

"What happened?" she whispers.

I glance over my shoulder and shrug with a nonchalance I don't feel. "Roadside bomb a long time ago. Didn't you notice the ones on my face?"

"Your thick, beautiful beard detracts from them."

"Yeah." I chuckle without humor. "That's the point."

"It's a sexy cover-up, Ragnar. Gives you a hardened, weathered warrior vibe," she calls to my back as I slip into the bathroom.

"I'm nothing more than a guy with a dog," I say behind the door, grabbing a couple of tissues and disposing of the condom. Running my faucet, I grab a washcloth and quickly clean up my face and then my dick before tossing the rag into the hamper.

I walk out to find Mari nearly dressed, her bra and tank top on, her jeans halfway up her thick thighs.

"Are you leaving?" I can't keep the surprise out of my voice.

She brings her eyes up to meet mine and at least has the decency to look ashamed. "I really should go."

The muscles in my jaw clench as anger rushes through my veins. Is it my scars suddenly turning her off or something else? Was I too rough? Too gentle?

Ah fuck. Who the hell knows?

"You don't have to." I self-consciously cover my dick with one hand while looking for a pair of shorts. "I'm cool with you staying... if you want."

Mari pulls her pants up and plops down on the edge of the bed, slipping her socked feet into her boots without lacing them up. "I think maybe it's better this way. Ya know?"

Finding a pair of shorts, I slide them on and then push my hair back from my face. "No, I don't know."

"Well, it's like you said. Cher and Vale are embarking on something big, presumably life-changing. How are they going to feel about their two best friends fucking?"

I don't know why, but her words are a slap to my battle-scarred face. Pressing my lips together, I say nothing, because there's not much I can say. She's basically parroting my words back to me from earlier.

"So, maybe it's best they never find out about tonight. We'll act like this never happened," she says as she scurries out of my bedroom and into the living room, where she at least has the decency to bend down and give Krieger a few gentle scratches behind his ear.

Never happened?

Never happened!

Clenching my jaw, I can't form words as rage blinds me. I follow behind her, saying nothing.

Not one fucking word.

She pats her pockets and glances around real quick as if to make sure she has all she needs. "This was fun."

"What was?" I grit out. "Nothing happened."

Sadly, she nods and plasters on a big smile as she opens my front door. "Exactly. Good night, Kemp."

I stare out the door as her taillights skirt the tree-lined street and fade out of view before closing and locking my front door.

What the fuck just happened?

I've never had a woman run so hot and then so cold in the span of a couple of hours.

Fuck hours. Minutes. It was minutes between us coming and her being dressed and out the door.

And we didn't exchange phone numbers, although I suppose that was not a mistake on her part.

Jesus.

An hour ago I would've said we were damn near perfect for each other. Yes, I desire something a bit more primal in the bedroom, but what I really want is passion, and I thought Mari had it in abundance.

And now? I have no idea what that was.

Talk about a mind fuck.

And something tells me she'll be plaguing my thoughts for a long time.

VETERAN
K9
TEAM
REPORTING
FOR DUTY

Chapter Four
Mari - Six weeks later...

"You're what?" My head snaps up at the same time I drop my passionfruit-flavored Vitamin Water.

Cher looks around the break room conspicuously before bending down to retrieve my forgotten beverage. "I'm pregnant."

"Oh. My. God." I stare at her blankly. "I'm not sure what to say."

"Congratulations work." Cher frowns at me, her feelings obviously hurt.

I throw myself at her, wrapping my arms around her waist that I now realize is housing my future niece or nephew. "I'm sorry, girl. This is just such a shock. If you're happy, I'm ecstatic."

She slips her arms around me, her voice shaking slightly. "I am happy. It wasn't planned, obviously, but I know it's right. Vale and I are having a baby... and it feels so perfect, I think my heart might explode."

I pull back to find her eyes welling with tears. "How far along are you?"

"Nearly six weeks, we think."

"We've only been home for six weeks." I point out.

"Exactly. I think the condoms in my nightstand were expired." She shrugs, a rogue tear rolling down her cheek.

"What did Vale say?" I have so many questions, I'm not sure where to start.

"He immediately dropped to his knees and pressed his lips to my belly before asking me to marry him."

"And?"

Cher smiles. "Mari, will you be my maid-of-honor at an impromptu backyard ceremony?"

I narrow my eyes conspiratorially. "Do I also get to be godmother as well as number one auntie?"

Cher chuckles, more tears rolling down her cheeks, which triggers an involuntary response from me as my own tears break free. "Of course!"

The more the reality of her changing world settles on me, the more excited I get.

Baby clothes.

Toddler toys.

Kids' birthday parties with pizza, cake and ice cream.

Christmas with Santa.

Goofy pictures with the Easter bunny at the mall.

Oh God. Now I'm excited!

"When's the wedding?"

"Well, that depends on what we can pull off as far as venues, but ideally it would be in the next two months while I can still take flattering wedding photos. I need some of your amazing logistics skills."

I grin wide, barely containing my joy. "You got them, girl."

As soon as the words are out of my mouth, Cher's phone rings.

"Hey, babe." Her face lights up and something clenches around my heart as I realize I'll be seeing Kemp soon. We've only seen each other once since I rebuffed his offer to spend the night and hastily retreated out the door before he could bribe me to stay with another orgasm.

Ugh! Why does he have to be so damn sexy?

There was something about his tender touches and offer to make me breakfast in the morning that set off the warning alarms in my head.

Danger! Danger! Danger!

I've never felt the desire to sink into a guy before like I did Kemp, and that alone means I need to stay as far away from him as possible.

Stay the night? No.

Grab breakfast in the morning? Hell to the no.

Both sound like things people building relationships do and I avoid that whenever possible. It's been hard as hell not to roll by his place in the middle of the night to get myself another taste of some of the best sex I've ever had in my life.

The one time I slipped was nearly three weeks ago. I'd gone out with a couple of people from work, had two shots too many and told myself to go straight home. Even though I walked out of his house without exchanging numbers—a hurtful statement being the last thing to fall from my tongue—that doesn't mean my mind hasn't been plagued with memories of that night. While we said this would be nothing more than pleasure—absolutely no expectations—I know it would be too easy to fall for his charms.

Except that night, my Jeep found its way to his front door.

And then I promptly embarrassed myself with my actions.

I practically pushed myself into his house and immediately dropped to my knees, daring him to fuck my mouth like the good little whore he knew I could be.

He'd opened the door with a tumbler of whiskey in his hand, his body freshly showered and flannel pajama pants slung low on his narrow hips. No words passed his lips and the shock on his face was quickly replaced by dark, brooding desire.

I think, if he hadn't been taken by surprise, he would've said no.

But he didn't. Instead, he fucked my mouth and then my pussy raw without uttering one word of praise—only filthy degradations and a round of well-placed spankings that get me hot thinking about them today.

If I liked him gentlemanly, having him vulgar was exhilarating.

The memories make me want to provoke him again and see what it would be like.

Don't get me wrong. I'm sure there's a time and place

for sweet, vanilla sex, but deep down, I crave darkness. I always have and I have no idea how to have it in a relationship.

Cher pulls her phone away from her face and covers it with her hand, pinning me with her expectant gaze and pulling me out of my memories that send tingles straight to my pussy.

"Hello? Earth to Mari."

"Yeah, what's up?" I plaster a smile on my face. "What's the hottie saying?"

She giggles, a light blush hitting her cheeks. Oh shit, I don't think I've ever seen my friend blush—or if I have, it's been few and far between—which confirms how absolutely head-over-heels in love with Vale she really is.

"He thinks we can use one of the new buildings for an impromptu wedding and reception on the property. He wants me to come out and look at it after work. Are you down for a road trip?"

"Sure. Let's do it!" I add a bit of enthusiasm to my tone. How will Kemp look at me after the last time we saw each other? After he fucked me good and hard—both of us coming twice before we finally collapsed. After I gathered my shit and walked out without giving him my phone number or a chance at building a friendship —again?

This time he had the last word, repeating the shit I said to him weeks prior. *"This never happened."*

Fuck me. Will Kemp be there today? I knew I'd have to face him again, eventually. No doubt at a BBQ or

Christmas party, but after the way we parted the last time, I'm not sure I'm ready for this.

Three hours later, I'm driving Cher out of town to the Veteran K9 Center. I've never been out here before, but it looks like it's in the middle of a transition. In the Army, I work in logistics, specifically supply, for a small security forces detachment. Cher is in administration, which means she is on bitch duty whenever we deploy—specifically, running an armory when there isn't paperwork to be done.

The sight of Kemp's gray Jeep in the parking lot makes my stomach drop. This would be so much easier if he were an ugly asshole. At least then I could deny my attraction and the fear of falling in love.

Dogs bark in the distance as the main door to the middle building opens and Vale walks out with a dazzling smile on his face. Cher all but jumps out and runs into his arms, the two of them a nauseatingly perfect picture of bliss.

Blah.

Slapping on a smile, I jump out and let my combat boots hit the gravel drive. Cher begged me to forgo changing, her excitement to get out here outweighing my need to present the tastiest morsel I know I can be. I grab a small notepad from my center console and approach the happy couple who are so wrapped up in each other they don't notice me.

"Hello, Hottie. Or do I have to call you Mr. Turner?" I flash him a playful smile. It doesn't matter if he's my best friend's man. My go-to personality with everyone, male and female, is flirty, unaffected, or snarling bitch. Few get my bitchy side because few deserve it.

Thankfully, Cher knows this about me and knows I mean nothing by it—so she doesn't bat an eye when they pull apart and face me.

"Hey, Mari. Thanks for driving my fiancée out. I want to take her to dinner before heading home."

"No problem." I wave to the buildings. "Let's take a look at what we are working with."

He nods, wrapping his arm around Cher's waist. "This way."

We walk to the northern-most building—one of three basic metal prefabricated structures built on healthy concrete slabs. Inside is bare, but relatively clean, with industrial-style fluorescent lamps hanging overhead. Honestly, it's close to the buildings we set up overseas. Basic, but utilitarian structures with endless possibilities.

"We were talking about setting up on one end, renting chairs and tables and the like," Vale says to Cher and me.

"And the like?" I grin.

"Uh, besides Janey, I work with all guys—most of whom haven't been married. They weren't very helpful with ideas outside of constructing a fully functional bar." He rolls his eyes and shakes his head.

I grip his forearm and squeeze. "Thank god you have me."

It's at that moment the exterior door opens, the setting sun in the west casting the figures in dark shadows. But there's no way to miss Kemp's imposing form as he fills the threshold, bringing up the rear.

I instantly go into full-on fun and flirty mode, pasting a huge smile on my face. "Who are your friends?"

Vale turns Cher to the group walking in and I realize she hasn't met them either. Or at least, I don't think she has. It's only been six weeks, and she hasn't mentioned a get-together or anything. If there'd been a party, she would have invited me.

At least, I think she would have.

A petite woman with a faint scar on her left cheek approaches with her hand out to Cher. "Congratulations. We are thrilled for you and Vale."

Cher blushes again and I'm struck with how fast things are changing for her... and for me.

My best friend is getting married. Where does that leave me?

"Baby, this is Janey, Linc, Barron and Karden. You already met Kemp." Vale points to each person and then pulls her even closer to his side. "Guys, this is my Cher and her best friend Mari."

I shake hands enthusiastically with Janey, trying not to ogle Linc, Barron and Karden—all of whom are hot as hell. Why didn't our K9 handlers in Qatar look like this?

My eyes skim over Kemp, who stands in the background with his arms crossed over his chest like a larger-than-life bronzed berserker watching over his fields of fresh kills.

No smile splits his lips.

No emotion passes at all.

Janey nods to the rank insignias on our chest. "Staff Sergeants. Are you lifers?"

Shrugging, I look at Cher and wonder what her answer will be now that she's pregnant and engaged. At one time we said we'd do our twenty, draw our retirement and travel the world together, but I guess that reality has morphed into a husband, kids and a white picket fence. "That's the plan."

"Well, I'm thrilled to meet fellow female military members. We can use some estrogen around here." She winks and steps aside while the other guys introduce themselves to Cher and then me.

Linc is just as flirty as he was the night we met, but his gaze holds no lusty passion, letting me know he's a lot like me—mostly talk. Karden nods and gives me a hardy albeit brief handshake, his plentiful black and gray tattoos casting him with a don't-fuck-with-me appearance. Barron is big and thick like a bear, but a casual sweetness oozes through his massive size.

Only Kemp gives off an air of nonchalance, as he doesn't make a move toward us.

I'm not sure what these guys have heard, if anything. I mean, it should be nothing—that was our agreement.

"So..." I clap my hands and spin around. "We can totally make this space work. I have a party rental hookup, so I'd just have to see what they have scheduled already. When do you want to host this shindig, and how many people are you thinking?"

As Vale and Cher rattle off family members and friends, I take surreptitious glances in Kemp's direction.

Man, he is fine, but obviously pissed about our encounters, if the glower is anything to go by.

Is it wrong that his anger only soaks my panties? Memories of him fucking my face while tears streamed down my cheeks, only to spin me around, yank down my pants and push me to my elbows before he plunged into me, making the lower half of my body tremble with need.

I should not taunt this man, but the sex is so damn good.

The guys excuse themselves and Janey leaves a few minutes later, leaving me, Cher and Vale behind.

"Three weeks from today." I nod. "I'll see what I can do."

Cher throws her arms around my neck and pulls me into her chest. "Thank you so much."

"Who will be your best man?" I ask, my voice muffled by her breasts.

Vale runs his hand through his hair. "Kemp will stand up for me."

Oh great. "I see."

"Is that a problem? He said you got along fine that night at the Last Stand."

"Uh, we did. Yeah. No problems on my end." I smile sweetly. My memories of him and the things we did are anything but sweet—except when he was sweet, which was what sent me running into the night.

"You should tag up with him before you leave tonight. He'll be on task to get you and the vendors access to the building before, during, and after the big day."

Exchange phone numbers with Kemp. Well, damn. "Okay."

"You hungry, baby?" Vale kisses Cher's temple, and something akin to jealousy skitters up my spine. He's so affectionate and loving, obviously one hundred percent enamored with her. Everything she deserves but didn't know she wanted. Before Vale, she wasn't looking for a boyfriend, much less a husband. How did she know he was the one? How has she accepted her world turned upside down so easily? She's my best friend, but this isn't something we've talked about before. Neither of us was fantasizing about our happily ever after.

"I am." She smiles at me. "Can you grab Kemp's information before you leave, or do you need us to go with you?"

"I'm good." I wave them away, shooing them toward the door. "Go eat. Feed my future niece or nephew."

That makes Cher giggle and Vale smile broadly like the new father he is about to be.

Behind their backs, I struggle not to roll my eyes. Don't get me wrong; I want my friend to be happy. But their giddiness borders on ridiculous.

Outside, Kemp is walking with Krieger to his Jeep, which I'm parked next to.

"Hey Kemp. Hold up." I yell with my hand in the air, proving to Cher that I'm all in on my maid-of-honor duties.

His spine stiffens as I approach, the gravel crunching underneath my combat boots. "What's up?"

I keep my voice bright for the audience within

earshot. "Vale thought we should exchange numbers, as you will help me get the vendors in and out of here around the big day."

He chuckles darkly as Vale and Cher enter their truck with Sookie and Strijker in the backseat and keeps his voice low. "Now you want my number?"

As soon as they pull out of the parking lot, I let my smile drop and narrow my eyes. "What do you want me to say? We said this would be pure pleasure and no expectations. Exchanging numbers, making dates, staying the night and breakfast in bed all lead to expectations."

"So instead you show up at my house drunk, demanding to be fucked like the good little whore you are?"

Something about the words rolling off his tongue causes my insides to clench. "You seemed to like it at the time."

"I've been walking around for weeks wondering if Vale was going to punch me in the face for treating his woman's best friend like I did that night."

I shake my head, my insides aflame with the memory of the hottest fuck I've ever had in my life, my voice quivering with renewed need. "You did nothing I didn't want you to do. Are you saying you didn't like it?"

"Of course I liked it. That's not the point," he hisses and slides his hand down his silky beard.

Karden, Linc, and Barron exit the building with their dogs in tow—a Belgian Malinois, Husky and older German Shepherd. They wave and Linc calls out,

"Going to stop at the Last Stand for a burger and a beer if you want to join us."

Kemp nods in their direction but doesn't commit to anything.

"Are you joining them?" I hope he says no. I really do. Arching my brow, my desire to poke him into a repeat of three weeks ago burns a hole in my panties. How can I tempt him to take control again like he did that night?

I want this man.

I want him to do filthy things to me.

And then I want him to send me home fully used and sated.

"I'm not sure." His eyes rake over me, sending a chill up my spine. Does he feel the vibe flowing between us? Does it turn him on as much as it does me?

Janey walks out with a Rottweiler at her side and stops short when she sees us. "I thought I was the last one."

"We're exchanging information for Vale's wedding and then we'll be on our way." Kemp takes a step back from me, his eyes glued to the cute female with blonde hair. His demeanor changes when she approaches, resembling the nice guy I met six weeks ago. "Everything locked up?"

"For now. I'm going to take a dinner break, run a few errands, and then come back for the night shift." Janey smiles at me.

"Night shift?" I ask.

"Yeah. We take turns staying one night a week out here when we have kennel dogs on the premises. There's a trailer in the back, but someday we'll have a two-bedroom apartment complete with a decent kitchenette." She shrugs. "At least that's the plan."

"You have big things scheduled for your little operation, don't you?" I notice the pride in her eyes.

"We do." She tilts her head in Kemp's direction, including him in her world.

We. I don't know why, but the word sticks out to me like a tacky dress at a sleek black-and-white party and makes me wonder what, if anything, there is between them.

"I've got to get on the road." She chucks Kemp on the shoulder and tilts her head in my direction before she and her dog slip inside her Dodge Charger. "See you tomorrow. Nice to meet you, Mari."

We watch as she drives away, but neither of us makes a move to pull our phones out of our pockets.

"Want to see the kennels?" Kemp says with a hoarseness to his voice, the words strangled.

VETERAN
K9
TEAM
REPORTING
FOR DUTY

Chapter Five
Kemp

Anger and sex have never mixed in my world, and yet Mari fills me with both.

I'm still angry over the way she left that first night.

Still furious—and turned on—by the way she stumbled up to my door the other night.

Still hard at the sight of her.

My body comes alive in her presence.

Need pulses through my veins and rushes straight to my dick as soon as her eyes meet mine.

She fills me with desire so primal that it scares me.

But what scares me more is how it seems to exhilarate her.

Could I have stumbled upon the one woman who craves the things I do and yet has no desire for a relationship?

Yeah, that's totally how fate likes to fuck with me.

"This way." I lead her into the building, disarming the alarm and turning off the playtime cameras in the facility. I don't need a recording of what I think we're about to do for my team members to stumble upon later.

Instinctively, I wrap my hand around the back of her neck without saying a word and guide her through the maze of offices into the training area beyond.

This is her chance to resist.

To call me on my bullshit.

To turn around with her fist cocked, ready to deck me for my domineering hand.

Instead, she melts into my hold and lets me maneuver her to the storage room beyond the artificial turf where we house agility equipment, tactical harnesses, bite suits and leather leads.

At the threshold, I let go and face her as her gaze takes in the variety of training equipment we use.

"What do you want from me, Mari?"

She brings her eyes up, a flash of sass and defiance glittering back at me. "I thought it was obvious."

"You want me to treat you like my personal fuck doll, while you treat me like your dirty secret," I state rather than ask.

The sharp intake of her breath gives me my answer.

"If you want my cock, Shorty, you are going to have to beg for it."

Mari's lips are set in a firm line. "I don't beg."

"We'll see." I narrow my eyes, a rush of forbidden power flooding my veins. My dick stands at attention, straining against my zipper as a battle of will commences between us. I've never engaged in this kind of power play, but I've often fantasized about it. "Take off your ACU top."

She hesitates for a second and then slowly undoes the buttons from the bottom to top before draping it on the edge of the table that I plan to bend her over before this night is done.

My eyes rake over her uniform. A sand-colored T-shirt stretches tight across full breasts. A tapered waist cinched by a khaki nylon belt looped through digital camouflage print trousers that do nothing for 99% of the population and yet cradle her sweet ass perfectly.

In all my years of active duty, I never fucked a woman who was wearing ACUs. I've been wearing my cammies while we mess around, but I've never had this fantasy play out.

Hell, I didn't even know this was a fantasy until now.

"On your knees," I say without a hint of warmth or playful tone.

Her eyes narrow and her lips part in protest.

I don't know what demon takes over, but I'm on her in point-two seconds, backing her up against the wall of leather and nylon leashes with my stomach pressed against her breast. When we met, she had a tumble of cute twists in her hair, but now her hair is smooth and pulled back into a low ponytail at the nape of her neck.

Perfect for me to handle.

I wrap my hand around her hair and pull back, forcing her eyes to lift to mine as I tower over her.

"You want to play games with me? I'll play. But we play them my way." I bend down and inhale her scent, my lips and beard barely skimming her neck, before I pull back to pin her in the eye. "On your knees, whore."

Her breasts heave and her eyes fly wide with that one word, but she drops readily to the ground anyway.

I take a step back but keep my grip on her hair and her eyes up at me. "What do you want from me?"

She moans softly. "I want your cock in my mouth."

"Just like the greedy little slut you are," I smirk, the words spilling out of my mouth easier than I would have expected. I've never talked to a woman like this before.

It's raw, carnal, and utterly filthy.

She loves it.

As do I.

"Yes," she whimpers, her eyes coming down to the bulge that is aching to be freed from behind my cargo pants.

"Undo my pants."

She reaches up with nimble fingers, unlatching my belt and sliding down my zipper. My cock springs free and bobs in front of her face in invitation.

She wraps her hand around my length and opens her mouth, but I pull her head back with a quick tug of her ponytail. "Beg."

"What?" She casts me an incredulous look.

"I want to hear from your lips how much you crave my cock. If you want me to be your dirty little secret while fucking you into oblivion, you have to beg me— right here, right now. Otherwise, grab your shit and get out."

She sets her jaw. "I'm not going to beg."

I let go of her hair and take a step back, pulling my cock free from her hand. I quickly tuck myself back into my shorts and shrug. "Then go home."

"Wait." A surprised gasp escapes her lips. Her eyes are wild as she looks up at me. "Please."

Satisfaction seeps out of every pore as I pull my dick out with one hand while wrapping my fingers around her throat with the other. I use my thumb to push her chin up and bend down to put my mouth over hers, planting a punishing kiss before pulling back with a sneer. "Was that so fucking hard?"

"You're kind of being a bastard," she pants right before I stand and shove my cock into her mouth.

"And you kind of fucking love it. I bet your panties are soaked right now." I grab her hair again and pull back enough to give her air and the freedom to dazzle me with her talented tongue. "Now suck me hard, suck me good, swallow every fucking drop I give you and maybe I'll let you come."

Mari works me in earnest, as if to prove a point—one I'm eager to learn. The harder she sucks, the closer I get to my release. I take over and grip the sides of her face, pumping my hips, and fuck her mouth until she completely submits and lets me chase my climax.

"Fuck." I grit my teeth as my balls tighten up and cum shoots down my shaft to paint the back of her throat.

Mari is a garbling, gagging mess underneath me when I pull back to let her breathe. She swallows hard and pants before lavishing my length again with her tongue. When I finally fall from her lips, I use my thumb to push a dribble of cum from her chin into her mouth. "Every fucking drop."

She sucks my thumb and then smiles at me—as if she knows something I don't.

Sassy little wench.

I want to chuckle.

I want to lighten the mood.

But this game feels too good to stop now.

Letting go of her hair, I wrap my hand around the back of her neck and lift her to her feet, pushing her ass against the giant wood table we use to fix harnesses and punch new holes into leather leads. "Drop your pants, Shorty. Show me how wet my pussy is."

"Your pussy?" she scoffs as if offended, and yet that doesn't stop her fingers from flying over her belt and undoing her buttons.

"Yeah, my pussy. When it's just you and me playing whatever sick, twisted fucking game this is, it's mine."

She pushes them and her panties off her hips without embarrassment, meeting my domineering tone with as much strength as her quivering thighs allow.

And that's just it.

Her legs are shaking with pent-up need and she can't hide that from me, no matter how much bravado she puts into her smart-ass mouth.

"Finger yourself." My heated gaze locks onto the glistening slickness coating her thighs and it takes everything within me to not drop to my knees and slide my tongue into her depths.

She's sinfully smart as she leans her ass against the

table and arches her pussy up, using one hand to spread open her thighs and the other to slip two fingers between her slick folds before plunging them deep inside her. All the while, she keeps her eyes on me, watching my face for a passing emotion I'm unwilling to give.

This woman is the sexiest, ballsiest, filthiest, most perfectly primal woman I've ever met—and she doesn't want anyone to know about us.

She pulls her fingers out of her cunt and brings them to her mouth. Before I can stop myself, my hand snatches out to grip hers and I yank her fingers from her lips to lavish them with my tongue. Her taste is sweet and tangy, like a sour apple candy soaked in whiskey and then rolled in sugar. Addictive and, on some level, absolutely horrible for me. "Turn around and bend over."

Mari gives me a self-satisfied smirk before turning her back to me and slowly lowering herself to the table.

I don't have the patience for her antics.

My control is crumbling by the second.

And then I remember a crucial detail that's going to fuck up at least some of our fun.

I flatten my hand between her shoulder blades, pressing her down on the table forcefully. "Tits and cheek on the table. Ass in the air."

She complies without complaint. Not that I think she minds one second of what's going on here.

Holding her down with one hand, I plunge two fingers into her sopping wet pussy, pumping them in and out with all the aggression I feel.

She's not a bitch and yet she angers me, filling me with feelings I can't quite express.

Am I actually mad? No.

Am I frustrated? Yes.

Am I turned on by her antics? Also yes.

Is this sustainable behavior? Probably not.

"You want me to fuck this tight pussy, don't you?" I damn near growl from somewhere low in my chest.

"Yes," she moans as I add a third finger and press the pad of my thumb against her asshole. I wonder if she's into anal? I've never done it, but am more than willing to try. With her, there might be nothing off-limits.

"You want my cock deep inside you, don't you?"

"Yes!" She gasps when I remove my thumb, spit saliva between her spread ass cheeks and speed up my machinations by rubbing my thumb even faster against the tight, puckered hole.

Damn, I guess she likes it.

"You want to come, don't you?"

"Please." Her cry is desperate as her pussy walls start to pulse around my fingers.

I pull my hand out and feed her my fingers, shoving them far down her throat. "We have a big fucking problem then, because I don't have any condoms, and the only way you are coming today is with my cock deep inside you."

Mari's primed body slumps on the table, and she lifts her head to look at me. "I haven't been with anyone besides you since before I left for the desert."

"What are you saying?" My dick throbs with the implications her words leave me.

Nobody but me, despite her avoiding me for weeks at a time.

This pussy really is mine.

"Please fuck me." Desperation laces her tone, and I swear I'm going to hell.

"Are you protected?" At this point, I don't recognize my voice. The sound coming out of me is from another dimension. Guttural and tortured.

Maybe I'm already in hell.

"Yes," she pleads.

I nod my head to a place above her. "Grip the table and don't let go."

Fuck me, now would be the time to lace her up with a pretty rope and bind her in place. But we're way beyond that as I fist my cock and line up with her weeping hole, sliding the tip through her slick wet lips. "Beg me to fuck this pretty pussy like the good little whore you are."

"Please, Kemp. Please fuck me like the good little whore I am."

"Close enough." I slam my hips forward and fill her, her cunt instantly clamping down with her release. Mari screams out, her body convulsing with the orgasm she's been desperate to have. I smack my palm flat on her plump ass until it's warm and rosy and pump my hips through her climax—bringing on another and then another—until I too am on the edge and ready to come. "You take my cock so well, just like a fuck toy should."

"Oh god." She whimpers the moment I release deep inside her.

The world stops spinning as my cock jerks one last time, my balls drained of cum. An eerie silence descends around us, the only sound being our ragged breaths—and I'm left with the question of what is going on between us. Are we grudge fucking without a legitimate grudge? Hate fucking even though we don't hate each other? Is this foreplay to something even more forbidden?

"This never happened," I say, my cock still shoved inside her.

She nods but says nothing.

No sassy retort.

No nothing.

I pull out and drop down to grab her pants bunched at her calves. Sliding them up her legs, I get a perverse sense of satisfaction that she's driving home with my cum dripping out of her, filling her panties, and sliding down her thighs. She'll be reliving every thrust until she's under a hot shower spray when she can finally wash her skin clean of me. But even then, I'm already inside her, marking her in the most primal way possible.

"Go home, Mari." I step back and tuck myself back into my cargo pants.

She pushes herself up but keeps her back to me, fastening her pants and belt before reaching for her ACU jacket. Taking in and letting out a deep breath, she shakes her head and rolls her shoulder before turning to look at me. There's a small scratch on her cheek, probably from rubbing against the wood table and I can't keep the concern from my face.

"Shit."

As if she can see her reflection, she touches her cheek and sighs. "Nothing a little cover-up can't fix. Don't worry, Ragnar. Our secret is safe."

I narrow my eyes and motion for her to precede me out of the storage room with a wave of my hand.

Krieger is lying in the middle of the play field when we exit. He raises his head and jumps to his feet to run over and greet us. I wonder what my faithful companion would think of the way I treated Mari just now. I doubt he'd like it if he grew protective of her.

We walk out the front door together, where I stop to re-engage the cameras and alarms.

Mari glances over her shoulder as she keeps walking, her strides long and sure for her height. Every step screams, Get.Me.the.Fuck.Out.of.Here. "Thanks for showing me the kennels."

Fuck me. She had to get the last sassy word in.

I really am in hell.

VETERAN
K9
TEAM

REPORTING
FOR DUTY

Chapter Six
Mari - Three weeks later...

"Ready?" I hand my best friend her bouquet of fall-colored flowers.

She nods, but her feet are firmly planted in place.

"What's wrong?" I've been so busy running around as the de facto wedding planner that I haven't had the time to be the best maid-of-honor possible for Cher today, and the death grip she has on me right now pulls my head back to the most important thing at hand—the bride. "Cher?"

"Tell me I'm not making a huge mistake," she whispers so our voices won't carry above the din of the crowd on the other side of the large, vacuous building. There are six-foot dividers and approximately sixty yards separating us from the rest of the party, where wedding guests anxiously await the bride.

"What?" I shake my head, trying not to think of the two dozen people waiting for our grand entrance. At this point, everyone has found their seats and Vale is standing at the front with Kemp by his side.

Oh, Kemp. I can't think about his sexy ass right now.

"Are you having second thoughts?" I whisper back.

"Yes. No. I don't know." She shakes her head, a rogue tear falling down her perfectly painted face. "I love him. I know I do. But this has happened so fast, and what if I'm making a huge mistake?"

I glance down at her relatively flat belly. "That ship has sailed, don't you think?"

She chuckles as another rogue tear falls.

I turn to a nearby table and grab an unopened box of tissues. "When did you start having these doubts?"

"Five minutes ago."

"Not last night, or this morning, or a week ago when his family came into town?"

Cher shakes her head, making the red tendrils of her updo bounce against her cheek. "No. Up until five minutes ago, I was absolutely positive this is what I wanted."

I smile, pulling a tissue out of the box and dabbing her cheeks. "It's just nerves, babe. That's all. Vale is a guy born of fairy tales. He's damn near perfect and desperately in love with you. If you haven't been having doubts all along, then I say get your ass out there and grab your happily ever after."

She takes a deep breath and lets it out slowly while nodding her agreement. "You're right. Of course, you are right."

"Of course I am." I toss my high ponytail over my

shoulder and give her a sassy bat of my eyelashes. "So, am I walking my sexy ass out there or not?"

"Start stepping." She gives me a real smile.

"You'll be thirty seconds behind me, right?"

"Yes."

I walk around the partition and signal the DJ to play our entrance song. Cher's father, Richard, approaches from his perch ten feet away with Sookie in her flower girl harness and leash at his side. I take her lead and accept a kiss from him—I've known the man since middle school—before starting my walk down the twenty-foot light gray runner I rented from the party supply store.

Everyone coos as Sookie prances, the overflowing baskets tied to her harness throwing flowers haphazardly to the ground.

I suppose it's no worse than what a distracted three-year-old would do given the ceremony.

For some reason, Strijker, who stands with Vale and Kemp, starts to howl, which causes Sookie to howl in response.

In this case, I have no idea what to do. I mean, can you stop huskies once they get going? Without the skills to handle this predicament, I proceed down the aisle as Sookie tells the assembled family and friends all of her opinions while Kemp does his best to calm Strijker. Most of the crowd laughs and snaps pictures of the show-stealing dogs, but a hush falls over everyone when Cher steps from behind the partition.

We've been tomboys our whole life, picking jeans and trainers over dresses and heels whenever possible. So, it surprised me when she picked a princess-style wedding dress with a full skirt and a sweetheart neckline for her big day. And then she put me in this gorgeous thing—a multi-hued, single-shoulder, split-thigh evening gown fit for a high society gala.

I have to admit; I feel glamorous in this curve-hugging dress and strappy heels with a tiny tiara comb at the top of my ponytail.

I take my place and avoid looking at Kemp while giving Sookie her one-word command. "*Sitz.*"

He and I had to interact one week ago when I brought the vendors out to show them the building and then again yesterday when they came out to set up. We never exchanged phone numbers, and I was forced to contact him by calling the center directly. I couldn't admit to Cher or Vale that we weren't in contact without giving something away, because I'm sure if I spent more than thirty seconds thinking about Kemp the blush on my cheeks would tell the world all they want to know and more.

Instead, I pretend like he doesn't exist.

Otherwise...

Dear god, the way that man plays my mind and body should be illegal. He's addictive, and it's taken everything within me to stay off his porch.

The wedding march starts, and Cher walks down the aisle on her father's arm with her eyes glued to Vale, a big smile on her face.

"She's beautiful, man," I hear Kemp say to Vale, who nods his agreement.

"I'm one lucky son of a bitch."

"Yeah, you are," I throw in, flashing him a teasing smile when he glances at me in surprise.

Kemp stares me down, his eyes filled with veiled annoyance, like I'm a petulant child he desperately wants to spank.

Mmmm. I do love his spankings.

All of us return our attention to the bride. Vale steps forward, shakes Richard's hand and then takes Cher's hand while I grab her bouquet. Around the room, half of the attendees are dressed in their Class-As with the exception of Vale and Kemp, who wear their Mess dress uniforms which, in my opinion, blow away any boring tuxedo. Add in the collection of combat medals, including several Bronze Stars and Purple Hearts, and this has to be the most awe-inspiring wedding I've ever been to.

The chaplain begins the ceremony, and I'm fumbling with two bouquets and a leash tied to a Husky who has decided she's tired of sitting in place. Glancing down at her as I try to adjust my grip, I hear Kemp say in a tight, low tone. "*Sitz*."

She immediately calms and snaps her attention to him, but I'm focusing on the warm flush of arousal damping my thong that his commanding tone brought on. My breath catches and nipples pebble in my tight bodice, and I can't help but glance in his direction, only to catch him looking back at me with full knowledge of his effect on me.

Kemp's mouth twitches as his gaze slides over me

like a hot caress filled with promises of what's coming, which only makes me squirm more under his assessment.

"Do you have the rings?" The chaplain's voice pulls me out of my filthy musings to the task at hand.

Kemp nods and pulls two rings out of his pocket, handing them to the officiant.

The ceremony continues, and minutes later, he pronounces them man and wife. Cher throws her arms around Vale's shoulders and the two of them kiss with the kind of passion I've never displayed in public.

How freeing it must be to openly show and share your love for another.

I can't even imagine.

For me, I'm too worried that one day I'll be made a fool of to risk ever allowing somebody to see me at my most vulnerable.

And to me, wearing your heart on your sleeve is about as vulnerable as you get.

Think about it. Everyone in this room right now knows that these two are head-over-heels in love with each other and would be absolutely crushed should anything break the bond they've sworn to keep before friends, family and god. If Vale ever betrays her—like my father did my mother, my uncles did my aunts, and even my brothers have their girlfriends—she'll know that all of these people witnessed her at her happiest and then at her most miserable.

Yeah, no. I can't even imagine.

And still, even as jaded by declarations of love as I

am, I can't stop the happy tears from rolling down my cheeks.

Cher turns to me and smiles so broadly that it jump-starts a tiny section of my cold, dead heart. "I love you, Mari. Thank you for being here for me today and every day."

I hand her the bride's bouquet. "I got you, girl. Always."

She and Vale walk down the aisle and through the tables towards the other end of the building while Kemp, Strijker, Sookie, and I bring up the rear. As soon as we pass the four rows of chairs, Kemp leans down and says something just for me to hear. "You look really beautiful."

"Something nice from your lips? Are you getting sentimental on me, Ragnar?"

"Are you wet for me underneath that long skirt, Shorty?"

I smirk, standing between the crowd and the private area we built in the back for Cher and Vale to have a few precious moments. "Maybe yes. Maybe no. Maybe it's not for you at all. There's a lot of eye candy here tonight."

"Careful," Kemp damn near growls, causing me to bring my eyes to his. "Poke at my jealousy with any of my brothers, and our twisted little game will no longer be a secret. I will bend you over and fuck you in the middle of this room just to prove my point. Do not test me on this."

The heat from his words floods through my body, bringing every nerve ending to life. I have to get out of here before I sink to my knees in front of him, my desire to submit to him unnatural given my past relationships.

I shove Sookie's leash into his hand and tilt my head towards the bartenders handling drink orders. "I'm going to check on everything."

For the next two hours, I avoid Kemp, although I can feel him watching me. Acting as part host, part social butterfly, I walk around and check in with my unit members, Cher's parents—who I hung out with more than my family in high school—and, as the night goes on and I get a couple of shots in me, the hotties from the VKC.

It's a little after seven and I'm sitting at a table with Janey, Karden, Linc and Barron, who tell me about their side hustle working Search & Rescue at Silver Mountain. It might be the liquor, but Linc has me in stitches as he regales us with a story about Florida coeds from last season while Barron sits by quietly and shakes his head in embarrassment. With Janey on one side of me and Linc on the other, my naturally flirty side comes out with story after story, keeping the group laughing. But when I slap my palm on Linc's forearm as he relays a hot tub incident involving a clogged jet and a rubber duck, warning bells sound in my head, causing me to glance around until I find Kemp standing with Vale's parents near the bar, his gaze narrowed in on where my hand rests on the muscular forearm.

I lock eyes with the man despite my best intention to ignore him all night.

Kemp shakes his head so subtly that I doubt anybody else sees it and then mouths silently, "Come here."

I start to stand before I realize what I'm doing and promptly sit before narrowing my eyes as my response.

He raises one eyebrow and mouths the word, "Now."

Linc places his hand over mine and pats it, bringing my attention back to the people at the table and the conversation at hand. I was so distracted by Kemp that I didn't even realize I still had my hand wrapped around Linc's forearm.

"Are you okay, Mari?"

"Oh yeah." I pull my hand back like his skin is on fire. "I think I'm going to use the ladies' room."

Janey pushes her chair back. "That's a good idea. I'll accompany you."

With Janey as my chaperone, we exit one metal building and enter the main office where there are multiple bathrooms with dual stalls. After we do our business, we're standing at the vanity washing our hands and touching up our make-up when I catch Janey staring at me through the mirror's reflection.

"So... you and Kemp, huh?"

"What?" I sputter, and pull the tube of red-tinted gloss away from my lips.

She continues as if she hadn't just dropped a megaton bomb in the tiny bathroom. "He's like a brother to me, you know. Actually, he's not like a brother. He is my brother. This is saying a lot, considering I have male siblings I rarely talk to. The three of us have known each other for a long time. Vale, Kemp and I went to boot camp at the same time and started AIT on the same day. We've been thick as thieves since day one, although

Kemp and I have always had a stronger bond." She smiles reflectively, like chasing a memory from a long time ago.

"I'd kill for that man and he'd kill for me."

I'm taken aback by the casual words that sound like a threat.

Was that a threat?

Is Janey LaVey threatening me?

I stare at her through the reflection as she recites what sounds like a well-practiced speech. "Nothing is going on between Kemp and me."

"Are you sure?" She flashes me a knowing smile. "You know, when we met three weeks ago, I had left to grab dinner and run a few errands. What you don't know is that I had forgotten my debit card on my desk. I was maybe five minutes down the road when I turned around and came back to find both of your cars still in the parking lot. Then I checked the security system via my phone and found that Kemp had turned off all the cameras in the facility. There's only one reason he would do that. I didn't want to disrupt you guys, so I figured out another way to pay for my food and drove into town."

Janey pulls a small tube of clear lip gloss from a pocket in her full skirt. She leans forward and applies a demure coat to her pouty lips before, once again, looking at me through the mirror's reflection. "He's a good man. Complicated, but you will never meet a man who will take better care of the ones he loves. I owe him my life and will do anything to protect him. Even butt into his personal business when he would never tell me willingly about what's going on."

She turns to face me. "I like you, Mari. You seem like a nice girl."

I shake my head and my voice is so small, I'm not sure she hears me. "I'm not."

She rests her hip against the countertop and pins me with her aqua-blue eyes. "Well, in the fourteen years that I've known Kemp, I've never seen him look at someone the way I've caught him looking at you. So, if you're not a good girl, maybe you should figure out how to become one, because I promise you he's worth it."

Why do I feel like I've just been dressed down by a superior officer?

"I'm not sure what you want me to say."

She shakes her head slowly. "I don't know what you can say. Obviously, I don't know what's really going on between you two and he's damn sure never going to tell me. Like I said, I'm his little sister, and he's not the kind of guy to talk about his sex life with anyone—especially me. What I can tell you is that if you are looking for a good man, he's standing across the room watching you with the kind of expression I've only ever seen on one man's face when he was looking at me."

"Your ex-husband?" She's mentioned being divorced over cocktails, although I really know nothing about her current relationship status.

Janey chuckles. "Sadly, no."

"Can I ask you a question?"

"Sure."

"What, in your estimation, qualifies a good man?"

Janey leans her ass against the counter and lets out a

deep sigh. "For me, he's a man that no matter how angry I make him, he never puts his hands on me."

That one comment has me glancing at the faint scar on her cheek and wondering about her past.

She continues. "He's confident in himself and isn't looking to me to pump up his ego or blame when things don't go his way. He wants to be there for me, take care of me—even if I don't need him to—and every time he touches me, I feel like I'm the most beautiful thing ever created. And he does all of this without saying a word."

I glance down at my strappy shoes. "Does a man like that cheat?"

"No. Never. His ego is whole without the attention of a woman and somehow, I am more than enough for him—even on the days that I don't think so."

Obviously, I've never asked my father or my uncles why they felt compelled to step out on my mother or aunts, but I have talked to the women in my life—some of whom forgave the cheating bastards, some of whom didn't.

Their answers never satisfied me.

My first boyfriend cheated on me by kissing Kathy Eves under the bleachers in our freshman year. The next day he dumped me and chose to take her to homecoming the following weekend.

I was humiliated.

My next boyfriend got caught making out at the overlook at Pickers Point with a girl I thought was my friend. Everyone in the school knew about it before I did, only adding to my embarrassment.

And then there was Trevor. The supposed one. The guy I lost my virginity to. The man who I thought I would marry after high school and live happily ever after with—forever. We talked about moving in together after graduation and what our lives would be like. We talked about our future together all the time. Then Natalie, a girl he worked nights with, showed up at my door six months pregnant. Turns out he was sleeping with a handful of girls, two of whom wound up pregnant within months of each other.

That had been the final straw. The moment when I knew no man could be trusted and I would never allow them to be complacent with my attention or affection.

Janey sighs, pushes off the counter and slips her hands into her skirt pockets. "Well, Mari. It seems to me like you and Kemp have some things to talk about. I hope we get to become friends. I really do."

She walks out and leaves me a bit dazed but with no confusion as to her feelings on the matter. The problem is, I don't know what I feel. Kemp is a great guy, and the sex is phenomenal. Instinctively, I knew I could come to him that night with my dark desires, even though we've never talked about such things.

Honestly, we could probably use some more talking and a tad less fucking—but he's so much fun to be fucked by.

Stumbling into a man's house and telling him to treat me like his whore—yeah, I've never pulled shit remotely like that before in my life. I've never trusted a man with that kind of control over me before. But with Kemp, I somehow knew it would be okay.

Is it because he's Vale's best friend and the accountability is there should he cross a line? Maybe.

Or maybe it's all Kemp.

Fuck me. This is so screwed up. I'm messed up. I haven't welcomed the hint of a relationship in so long, I wouldn't even know how to open myself up to one.

But if Kemp is half the good guy Janey says he is, maybe I need to try.

VETERAN
K9
TEAM
REPORTING
FOR DUTY

Chapter Seven
Kemp

I've spent the last ten weeks at war with myself.

The brief time I've spent with Mari has been complicated and exhilarating.

She's the devil on my shoulder—her slightly masochistic need speaks to the sadistic desires I don't completely understand. They bother me, especially since I don't get to participate in any kind of aftercare. The things I say to her, the roughness with which I handle her —I fucking love it.

I want and fantasize about more.

Exploring more.

Delving deeper into this taboo world that she also seems to crave.

Hell, it gets me hard thinking about it.

But when she doesn't allow me to make sure she's okay afterward, she leaves me in limbo.

I sit in my office with the lights off and my eyes glued

to the door. What the fuck are they doing in there? As soon as I saw Janey walk out of the reception with Mari, my hackles rose and I knew my friend was up to no good.

Finally, Janey walks out of the bathroom, her eyes coming directly to me even though I'm cloaked in darkness. "Party over?"

"It's winding down," I say softly.

She walks into the office and leans her back against the door. "Mari seems nice."

I arch my brow. "Does she?"

Janey chuckles. "She told me she's not."

Shrugging, I push my ass off the edge of the desk and roll my shoulders. "I wouldn't know."

"Oh?" Janey glances over her shoulder as Mari exits the bathroom and heads back to the reception, bypassing us completely. "Maybe you should talk to her?"

"She doesn't want to talk to me. Hell, she doesn't want to be seen with me." The words slip out before I can stop them and Janey meets my statement with a raised eyebrow.

"She said this to you?"

"Not in so many words."

"Sounds like the two of you need to use your words instead of whatever communication method you've been using to date." She smirks.

I narrow my eyes. "Don't go there."

Janey shrugs. "It would be perfect for the two best friends of the bride and groom to end up together. You can get together and do BBQs and shit."

"Janey LaVey, are you playing matchmaker?"

"No. But I wouldn't mind seeing you happy."

I roll my eyes and step out of the shadows, glancing into the customer area outside of our offices and to the doors beyond. "I'm happy."

"With a woman, Kemp."

Yeah, I need to shut this conversation down right now. "I tell you what, brat. I'll put myself out there when you do."

"That's not fair, and you know it," she hisses under her breath.

"It's been over three years, Janey." I shove my hands in my pockets. "It's time."

Janey shakes her head and shoves past me. "And to think, I told Mari you are a good man."

I watch her retreating back and wonder—am I a good man?

I walk back into the big metal building to find Cher and Vale dancing on the makeshift dance floor. Mari is talking to the DJ, while my team is at the bar grabbing the last round of drinks. Sliding up to the counter, I order a Maker's Mark on the rocks and turn my attention to the couple lost in their own little world. I've never seen Vale like this—not even with Nora—and I'd thought he'd been pretty happy back then.

Did he, on some level, know that she wasn't his happily ever after?

What about Cher is different?

When she came back from her deployment and the universe threw them together via a precocious Husky named Sookie, Vale had claimed it was fate. I, of course, shit all over that idea and pissed my friend off in the process.

Now here we are, ten weeks later, and he's married with a kid on the way. Maybe the universe is involved? Either way, he's so fucking in love with Cher, I don't think he'd be able to breathe without her.

Nora crushed his ego, but Cher would destroy his will to live.

And yet, there is something infectious about the love radiating off of them. It's hypnotic to watch, seeping into my skin and rushing through my veins to infuse every inch of my body with a longing I've never felt before.

Do I want this for myself?

I never have before.

I glance over at Mari, who is watching me with renewed interest reminiscent of the first night we met. Lifting my glass, I send her a silent toast and then tilt my head toward the dance floor.

Her lips twitch, and she gives me a small nod.

Tossing back half of my drink, I set it down and avoid eye contact with any of my team members as I walk to the edge of the dance floor to meet Mari and offer her my hand. "Is it appropriate for the best man and maid-of-honor to dance with the bride and groom?"

"A tornado could roll through here and I don't think they'd notice." She snorts, placing her fingers in my palm. "Do you know how to slow dance?"

"What's there to know?" I pull her into my arms, placing my free hand low on her back before gliding her around the edge of the dance floor.

"Oh my, Ragnar. You've got some moves." Mari smiles up at me and I swear it does something to my insides. "I can't believe you cut your beard for the wedding. That's serious dedication to your friend and the uniform."

Shaking my head, I inadvertently catch Janey's eye across the dance floor. She's got a shit-eating grin on her face and part of me desperately wants to flip her off. "I didn't cut it. It's rolled up under my chin."

"Oh, thank god. I would have missed it."

I smirk. "What would you have missed about it?"

She giggles, but doesn't answer the question. "You look very handsome in your Mess dress."

"And besides the bride, because it would be wrong not to make her number one on her wedding day, you are the most breathtaking woman I've ever laid eyes on."

Mari takes in a deep breath, her breasts heaving against the tight bodice of her dress. "I can't tell if I like you sweet and flirty, but I know I like you rough and filthy."

"Both men are me, although I've never shown someone the side of me that you seem to crave."

"Never?"

I shake my head and spin her once for good measure.

"That side of me is just for you. Tell me, Mari. Why don't you want to be seen with me?"

"What are you talking about?" Her brow furrows.

I lean down and put my mouth over her ear. "You love my cock. Can't deny that after the way you've dropped to your knees so many times to worship him. And if I remember correctly, you like my mouth on you, too."

She shivers, her body melting into my hands, but says nothing.

No denial.

No witty comeback.

"And yet, you've avoided giving me your phone number for two months. Is it me or all men in general?"

"Why do you need my phone number?" Her voice is breathy, my words affecting her more than I thought.

"How else would I ask you out on a date?"

My words are a splash of ice water and seem to wake her right up. She pulls her head back and looks me in the eye. "I thought we were going for casual?"

"That was the agreement when our friends were starting their relationship, but considering we're at their wedding, I think we're beyond that. Besides, no expectations doesn't mean fuck buddies, does it?"

"It does in my world," Mari says matter-of-factly. "I know this sounds cliché, but it's not you. It's me. Can't we just have fun without getting emotional?"

We've stopped moving, an epic stare-down playing out between us. I'd love nothing more than to drag her off this dance floor and back into the storage room, spanking her ass until she spews all the real thoughts running through her head. What's she hiding from that something as simple as a date scares the shit out of her? I've never met a woman more resistant to getting to know me in my life. I'm usually the one slow-rolling things to the point that the women lose interest and move on.

Mari might be the one to break the cycle, if I can only get her to let down her walls the tiniest bit.

It's only when I realize that people are staring that I yank her back into my arms and start swaying on our feet again, practically dragging her with me. "Do you really think what we do so well together is devoid of emotion? Rage fucking, or whatever the hell is going on between us, is overflowing with pent-up feelings let loose in the form of aggression and sex."

"You don't want to date me." There's a bitterness to her tone.

"Yeah, I do." We stop dancing and move to the corner of the floor when the DJ changes to something with a faster tempo. Our conversation is about to be cut short by the bride and groom approaching us.

Mari glances at them and then lowers her voice. "Well, maybe I don't want to date you."

"Why not?" I ground out through clenched teeth.

"If I don't date you, then I don't have to worry about falling for you." Mari hisses and then throws her arms wide to pull Cher into a big hug. "Congratulations!"

Her words hit me like a sledgehammer, and a need to

make her mine fills me. I have to persuade her to give me a chance and if I can't obliterate the walls surrounding her heart; I need to convince her to at least give me the key.

"You okay?" Vale eyes me curiously.

"Ready to get out of this suit, man."

He chuckles. "Yeah. You are way too big to be confined by polyester. I'm surprised you haven't stripped down to your undershirt yet."

Ironically, the groom discarded his coat an hour ago while leaving his bowtie hanging loose and the top buttons of his shirt undone. At some point, he also took off his cufflinks and rolled his sleeves to mid-forearm—all military decorum abandoned.

"I can maintain some semblance of civility when absolutely necessary." I snort, trying not to watch as Mari and Cher retreat to the privacy screens we set up in the back.

Vale follows my eyes. "You and Mari seemed to be having an intense conversation."

"We were discussing Viking folklore."

"Really?" Vale raises his brow, wordlessly calling bullshit.

"Yep."

He stuffs his hands in his pockets and we walk to the table where our teammates sit, smart enough to drop the topic—at least for now. I grab the last of my Makers Mark and toss it back while Vale fist bumps Barron, Karden, and then Linc. "We're about to get out of here. We still have some packing to do before we head out tomorrow."

Janey nods. "We'll close down the party for you."

He turns to me. "You got Sookie and Strijker, right?"

"Yep."

"Thanks, brother. I owe you." As if he's completely in tune with her, his head snaps up as Cher walks around the partition wearing a long cream cable-knit sweater dress with pale gray knee-high boots. Mari walks behind her wearing jeans and a baggy pink flannel shirt with her hiking boots.

Damn, I really wanted to fuck her while she was wearing those sexy strappy heels.

"I guess the party's over." I sigh and slide my hand over the knot in my beard. Absent-mindedly, I unfurl it as I note Mari once again doing everything she can to avoid eye contact.

Well, that's not going to work for me.

Vale holds his hand out to Cher. "Let's make the rounds and say good night. We'll see you guys in a week."

As the newlyweds exit the building with most of the wedding guests in tow, I turn to my teammates. "You guys can take off. The vendors will be out tomorrow to pick up their shit. Isn't that right, Mari?"

She nods, bringing her eyes warily up to meet mine. "Ten o'clock."

The DJ walks up behind her, wrapping a cable around his forearm as he approaches. "Hey, Mari. I'm done packing up and was wondering if you'd want to grab a drink with me in town?"

Her eyes grow wide as she turns from me to face him, but before she can get a word out, a territorial growl rips from my throat. "She's not available tonight, or any night in the foreseeable future."

He blanches, his eyes moving from me to her and back to me. "Sorry, man. I didn't know."

From behind me, Linc laughs while Karden mumbles under his breath. "That just fucking happened."

I don't turn to look at them. Instead, I wait for Mari to spin on me and unleash a round of protests on how I had no right to say that, or how dare I speak for her, or go fuck myself.

Something.

Instead, the look on her face is a mix of shock and pure, tortured arousal. Her dark eyes dart over my shoulder, presumably to Janey, before coming back to meet mine. She lowers her voice to not make a scene as my teammates move away from us—chairs sliding across the floor as jackets are pulled on and the deep timbre of their voices fades away.

"What the hell was that?" she whispers.

I lower my head and put my face in front of hers. "It's me ending this fucking game between us, Shorty. You're too fucking stubborn for your own good, and I'm not waiting for you to come to me anymore. Instead, I'm going to tell you what to do."

"What am I going to do?" She lifts her chin and puts her hands on her hips in challenge.

A sinister smile spreads across my lips. "You're going to show up at my house at nine p.m. wearing your dress and heels with an overnight bag in your hand. I want you to pack your Treks and a pair of stretchy yoga pants with an oversized sweater for tomorrow and whatever products you need to start your day."

She shakes her head. "I'm not staying the night with you."

"You are."

Her brow furrows. "Why do I have to put my dress back on?"

Leaning forward, I slide one hand around her waist and pull her body flush to mine while capturing her earlobe between my teeth. "Because I want to fuck you with that dress hiked up around your waist after I tongue your pussy and lap up your juices with those strappy high heels digging into my back."

Mari hisses, her body trembling in my arms. "Fuck me."

"Exactly." I pull back to look her in the eye. "I'm making your body promises I have every intention of keeping. Do not make me come looking for you, Mari. It would be a mistake to think I don't know where you live. My house. Nine p.m. Overnight bag. Any questions?"

She shakes her head.

"Is there anything left to do here before we leave tonight?" I pull back and glance around the now empty room. The DJ's shit is gone, and the bartender locked up the rolling cart full of liquor to be picked up tomorrow. The cake table needs to be cleaned, but I figure we can deal with that in the morning. It's cold enough outside to turn this building into an icebox once we turn the heaters off.

She shakes her head. "I guess not."

"Good." I press my lips against hers, holding the chaste kiss until her lips soften against mine. "I'll see you in an hour."

VETERAN
K9
TEAM
REPORTING
FOR DUTY

Chapter Eight
Mari

I show up at 9:15 pm in my dress and heels but leave my overnight bag in my Jeep out of spite.

Normally, I hate being told what to do, but the no-nonsense demands rolling off Kemp's tongue had my pussy clenching in anticipation.

Our bodies are completely in tune. Why can't I get my mind and heart on board?

I didn't mean to let my secret slip on the dance floor tonight. It came from somewhere deep within me and until it spewed out of my mouth, I didn't know that was what was holding me back.

If I don't date you, I don't have to worry about falling for you.

The guys I've dated as an adult were men I could easily walk away from. Casual dating and decent sex are comfortable for me. But Kemp has an intensity to him, even when he's saying nothing at all.

Especially when he's saying nearly nothing at all.

The door opens as I step up on the stoop. Kemp stands there in a plain white T-shirt and his mess dress trousers, his feet bare and hair and beard loose. His ice-blue eyes scan me from head to toe, settling on my empty hands. "Where's your bag?"

"I'm not staying the night," I say with even less conviction than earlier.

"It's in your Jeep." He glances down at his watch. "And you're late."

"I'm not one of your dogs, Kemp."

"No, you're my woman and fucking more obstinate than any pup I've ever cared for."

The ease with the way he claims me is unnerving, but of course, I can't let the puppy comment slide. "Are you comparing me to a dog?"

He slides his hand down his face and tugs on his beard, which I find unbelievably delicious. "Are you starting a fight with me so we get right down to grudge fucking each other's cares away?"

Damn. He's got me figured out.

Still, I can't stop the smirk from tilting up the corners of my mouth.

Kemp's hand snatches out and wraps around the back of my neck, pulling me forward. "Get your ass in here, Shorty."

He pulls me into his chest and places a chaste kiss against my lips, and yet it sends shivers through me all the same.

"Take a seat." His eyes direct me to the sofa. "And give me your keys."

"What keys?" I bat my lashes.

"Your Jeep keys so I can grab your overnight bag." He lets me go and holds out his hand.

Sighing, I give him my keys and take a seat. Something tells me it's futile to fight him tonight. I don't have the energy to resist him and he seems determined to make his point.

Minutes later, he walks back in with my duffle bag and sets it down in the hallway. He grabs two whiskeys off the counter and hands me one before taking a seat next to me. "Tell me about yourself, Mari."

I take a sip and lean back, crossing my legs and allowing the slit in my gown to split open to high on my thigh. His eyes flicker down and an appreciative smile appears on his face.

"What do you want to know?"

"Do you have any siblings?"

"Two younger brothers. You?"

He takes a drink and sets it down, pushing the coffee table back from the sofa. Kemp drops to his knees in front of me, sliding his palm up the outside of my thigh.

So, that's the game we're playing. The more I open up, the more he rewards me with the touch I crave.

"A little sister, but she died ten years ago." He presses a kiss to my knee.

My heart clenches with this one statement and I forget all about the game.

Leaning forward, I set my drink down and cup his face in my hands. "I'm so sorry. What happened?"

His eyes are glacier waters on a stormy day. "Car

accident. Her boyfriend was driving and lost control, sending them off a bridge. I'm not positive it was an accident."

"You think he committed suicide and took her with him?" I'm shaken by his story and the guarded way with which he tells it.

He nods. "Stories came out at her funeral. A lot of questions and accusations from her college friends, but no physical proof of his abuse. Not that it mattered. She was gone and there was nothing I could do about it."

"Still, I'm sure not knowing has been torture," I say while rubbing my thumbs over his cheekbones.

Kemp uncrosses my legs and then wraps his hands around my ass, pulling me forward on the couch cushion. "Do you talk to your family?"

"Yes, although we aren't necessarily close. I check in on my mom and dad a couple of times a month and see my brothers maybe once a quarter, even though we all live in town." The words come out easier than I would have expected, considering I rarely share things about my personal life. "Cher has been my family since high school. Her parents have been my parents too, and I probably slept at their house as much as my own starting our sophomore year."

"I believe family is who we choose more than who we are born to." Kemp separates my knees by pushing his wide chest between my thighs. He kisses my lips softly and leans his forehead against mine. "Thank you for sharing a piece of yourself with me."

I bite my lip. "It's hard for me."

"I understand. It's hard for me too." He kisses me more forcefully, his tongue sliding between my lips—dancing and tangling with mine until I'm clutching at his T-shirt and pulling it over his head.

It seems like Kemp is going to be gentle with me and I have to admit, that coupled with the peek into my personal life makes me twitchy. A desire to flee bubbles in my belly, but then he surprises me by standing up and hauling me over his shoulder in a caveman's hold.

I squeal and then giggle as he walks into the dining room, where a large oak table takes up much of the space. He sets me on the edge and takes a step back, his eyes raking over every inch of me.

"I understand trust is earned and for you, not given easily. I'm asking you to give me a chance to earn that trust."

"What did you have in mind?"

He glances at the table to the left of me, causing me to swing my eyes in that direction. Next to me are leather cuffs and a shiny red cotton rope.

I suck in my breath and swing my eyes back to him. "You want to tie me up?"

"Restrain your hands for today. Eventually, I'd love to learn the art of Shibari with you, but we'll take it slow and build that trust."

Tentatively stroking the rope, a small thrill shoots through me. I've always wanted to trust someone enough to give up control and let them tie me up. Kemp has been the closest I've come in many, many years. I've trusted him to take care of my body and treat me like the fuck doll he calls me, but even with me on my knees, choking on his cock, I knew I could break away.

This is the next step.

I pick up the cuffs and inspect them. They are legit. Thick leather, stiff with lack of use.

"Have you done this before? Used these cuffs on someone else?" Jealousy laces my tone, but I don't care.

"I bought them after our tryst in the storage room, hoping to use them with you."

I don't know why, but this admission thrills me. "I've never done this before."

"Me neither, but I've always wanted to and you're the first woman I've ever thought I could do it with."

"So you're trusting me as much as I'm trusting you?"

"Basically."

I hand him the cuffs and then offer him my wrists like a well-worn criminal. "How do you want me?"

Kemp takes the cuffs, his eyes sparkling with mischief. He wraps his hand around my throat and uses his thumb to push up my chin, hovering his lips against mine. "I knew you were fucking perfect for me."

"I don't let just anyone call me a whore, Ragnar." I stick out my tongue and lick the seam of his mouth.

A deep rumble comes from his chest and a territorial growl laces through his words. "No man better ever talk to you the way I do, because you're mine and I will gut anyone who thinks otherwise."

Kemp claims my lips in a punishing kiss, the gentleness from earlier gone. "Lie back and put your hands above your head."

I do as he says, stretching my arms above my head. He rounds the table and grabs a hold of my hands, pressing tender kisses to my palms before wrapping each wrist in leather. Anticipation ratchets up my excitement and arousal drips out of my pussy with the click of the buckle cinching my wrists together. I glance up at him as he unties the red rope and loops it into an intricate slip knot.

"You look like you know what you're doing." I'm breathless, my fantasies slowly rolling into reality.

"I know how to tie knots." He grins as he loops the rope between my wrists and cinches it down. "How does that feel?"

I wiggle my fingers and pull slightly against the restraint. "It feels good."

Kemp grins down at me like a kid checking over his favorite toy. He glides his fingertips over my breasts, pushing down the one side of my dress not held up by a shoulder strap. "I should have stripped you first, but the vision I have of bending you over with your skirt draped around your waist is too good to ruin."

He pinches my nipple between his thumb and forefinger until I hiss against the delicious pain.

"Oh," I moan, flexing my fingers against my binds.

Kemp chuckles, continuing his sweet caress down my body until he once again is at the bottom of the table between my feet. He slides his hands up my legs, pooling my skirts high on my thighs. "How attached are you to these?" His finger brushes against the wisp of fabric between my legs.

"Not very."

I barely have the words out before he rips them off of me, the tiny lace thong shredding easily in his big hand.

The gasp escaping my lips turns into a low moan as Kemp slides two thick fingers inside of me. "How long have you been wet for me? Ever since I told Sookie to sit in that commanding tone? I bet that spoke to you on some baser level, didn't it?"

"Yes."

"Deep down you know you're my little whore and no one else's, isn't that right?"

"Yes."

Kemp pulls his fingers out of me and replaces them with his mouth. He puts my feet with their dangerously sharp and pointed heels over his shoulders and proceeds to tongue fuck my pussy, banding my waist with his forearms. I writhe underneath his face, bucking my hips to chase the orgasm I've been flirting with for the last two hours.

"You want to come, Shorty?" Kemp stops right before I spill over the edge.

"Yes!" I gasp.

"Whose name are you going to scream when you do?"

"Yours," I whimper, desperate for release.

"That's right. Because this pussy is mine. Your orgasm—mine. And soon your heart—Will. Be. Mine." No sooner are his words spoken than his mouth is back on me, tongue inside me, and within seconds my orgasm comes crashing down.

"Oh fuck, Kemp!" Any residual strength I had to resist him melts away, the walls around my heart not exactly crumbling, but cracking open for the first time in twelve years.

Is there a possibility he'll hurt me? Sure.

Is he worth the risk? I hope so.

I feel like he gets me. He seems to understand that he'll have to coax the personal stuff out of me, rewarding me with tidbits of his own life in return. And when it gets too heavy, he knows I need him to get me out of my head.

No man has ever been in tune with me. I didn't give them a chance, and they didn't try.

But I can't resist this man anymore. I want him too badly.

Janey's words ring through the post-orgasmic fog clouding up my brain.

He's a good man. Complicated, but you will never meet a man who will take better care of the ones he loves.

I hope she's right.

VETERAN
K9
TEAM
REPORTING
FOR DUTY

Chapter Nine
Kemp

Mari would kill me if I admitted the moment I knew how I would make her mine.

It was when I caught her visceral reaction to the quick audible correction I made to Sookie's behavior. Mari is a woman who, when necessary, needs a man who can get her out of her head. Any kind of tenderness between us seems to make her overthink things, but an unfettered, primal touch pulls her right back out.

That is something I can do—for both of us.

Of course, Janey's little pep talk solidified my thoughts. Although she's wrong about one thing, using our words is only half the answer.

Mari and I are connected on a baser level, one that goes beyond verbal expression. Her body tells me much of what I need to know. She desperately wants to trust someone with not just her body, but her mind and her heart.

Only she doesn't know how.

That's a feeling I understand.

Together, we're going to learn how to trust each other with all of ourselves.

I circle the table and lean over her head, kissing her deeply. She kisses me back like a woman half out of her head, sated but eager for more. "I love the way you come for me."

"I love the way you make me come." She smiles lazily at me.

I catch her bottom lip with my teeth, tugging hard enough to cause a second of pleasurable pain before pulling my head back to pin her with my no-nonsense glare. "I'm going to loosen the rope, but keep the cuffs on, pick you up, and then bend you over the edge of this table. I'm going to fuck you raw and hard like my whore wants and then I'm going to strip and untie you, take you to my bedroom, where you will strip me. Then you're going to ride me until we're both too sated and tired to keep our eyes open. Got it?"

She nods, her eyes sparkling with renewed interest.

I loosen the rope, giving it another two feet of slack. I want those sexy heels planted firmly on the ground, but her body and arms pulled taut across the table where she has no choice but to lie her chest and face flat against the hardwood grain.

Back at her feet, I position her like I want her, flipping her skirt up over her perfect ass. "Fuck, I wish I took erotic photos because this is an image I want hanging over my bed."

I slip my fingers inside her, my thumb circling over

her puckered hole. "Have you ever been fucked in the ass, Mari?"

Her shoulder bunch, the tension racing through her body, causing every muscle to flex. "No."

"Do you want to?" I slide my free hand up her spine in soothing circles. "Not now, but someday?"

She relaxes under my touch. "Maybe someday. Are you into that?"

"I've never done it. Never really wanted to. But I like the idea of exploring each other everywhere in every way." I rotate my hand and stroke her G-spot. She gushes with the motion, her body primed for my cock. "I want nothing off limits between us. You are mine and I am yours. Do you understand me?"

"Yes." Her voice quivers as her pussy tightens around my fingers.

"Not yet." I pull my hand free and unzip my trousers, freeing my cock. Gripping him with one hand, I slide the head through her arousal and then thrust my hips forward, burying myself balls deep. She comes immediately, her cunt clamping down and pulsing to milk my balls dry.

But I'm not ready yet and pump my hips through her climax, bringing on another and then another for her before I'm on the verge of coming. "I love how well you take my cock. It's like your pussy was made for me."

"Yes!" she cries out as I slam my hips forward one last time, my cock jerking as thick ropes of cum shoot out of my dick into her pulsating pussy.

Once I'm drained, I slump forward and loosen my

punishing grip on her hips. I press a gentle kiss against the middle of her back and pant for breath. "Fuck, Shorty. You wear me out."

She groans as I slide out of her, but otherwise says nothing. Tucking myself back into my briefs, I untie Mari and pull her into my arms, carrying her like a bride to my bed. I stand her up, pull off her dress and then lie her down, unbuckling each heel before bringing her feet up on the mattress. Her gaze is glued to me, but otherwise, she is quiet, reflective and possibly too far inside her own head.

"What are you thinking?"

Shaking her head, she grants me a small smile. "I'm trying not to."

I slip off my trousers, climb into bed, and pull her onto my chest. "I don't know if anyone got a chance to tell you today, but you did a great job pulling together Cher and Vale's wedding. It was really beautiful, given the location."

She smiles, her breath tickling my pecs as she traces the ridges in my abdomen. "Thank you. Honestly, now that it is over, I'm exhausted."

"You should be. You worked your ass off." I slide my hand down her back and pinch her ass. "Of course, you could have had more of my help if you'd called and asked."

"Yeah, yeah." She smacks my stomach, making me grunt and pull her closer. After a few minutes of silence, she tilts her head up and looks me in the eye. "Don't break my heart, okay?"

The world stops spinning as the gravity of her question—no, her declaration—hits me.

She's accepting me... this... us.

I kiss her forehead, the tip of her nose, and her full lips. "Never."

Two weeks later...

"Hey, Shorty," I say as soon as Mari answers the phone. She's spent every night in my bed since the wedding and even brought over a couple of things, so she doesn't have to wear my clothes on the weekends when we get to sleep in. Not that I mind her wearing my T-shirt, especially when that's all she's wearing.

"How's my favorite beard?"

"Wishing you'd take him for a ride."

"Mmmm." She giggles, the noises of her coworkers packing up for the day filling in the background.

I mock-salute Linc and Barron, both of whom are in a hurry to get out of here after their weekend search and rescue stint up on Silver Mountain. "You remember that I'm sleeping out at the VKC tonight, right?"

Before making it official with Mari, I used to take more than my fair share of shifts out here, considering I didn't have anything else better to do. I mean, Krieger and I can train, shit, shower, and sleep here just as easily as we can in town.

Now, I have a reason to go home every night and with Vale newly married, Linc, Barron, Karden and Janey have had to pick up the slack.

"I remember. I'll miss you."

"I'll miss you, too."

"Do you want me to bring you dinner?"

"No. I've practically held you hostage at my house the last couple of weeks and you said you had a ton of chores to get done."

"I really do. I have laundry, grocery shopping, dusting... plus—" she cups the phone so no one else can hear her "—my pussy can use a break."

A self-satisfied grin spreads across my lips. I dip my head and lower my voice, even though the only other person here is Janey, but she's in the other room. "Are you saying I've fucked you like the good little whore I know you can be?"

Mari laughs out loud. "You know you have."

"Yeah, but I also kiss it better afterward."

To that, she sighs. "Yeah, you do that, too."

"Don't tease me." The words rumble out of my chest, but it's too late. Talking to and thinking about her makes me hard.

"I make no such promises. I'll call you later and tell you a sexy bedtime story." I hear her closing desk drawers and grabbing her purse and keys.

"Can't wait, Shorty. Go take care of your chores and I'll talk to you tonight." I love you is on the tip of my tongue—it's always on the tip of my tongue—but I swallow it down. The last thing I want to do is scare her off with such a bold statement.

"Well, well, well." Janey leans against the doorjamb into my open office with a pizza in her hands. "I never thought I'd see the day."

I set my phone down and roll my eyes. "Shut up."

She smiles but says nothing.

"I thought you were on your way home?" I stand and stretch my arms overhead. There's not a lot to do out here at nighttime, but we have internet, so I plan to binge a couple of shows on the History Channel and rack out for the night. While I don't like the idea of a night without Mari in my arms, I could use the sleep.

My cock won't let me get eight hours when she's in proximity.

"I thought we could bullshit like old times. It's been a while."

"Bullshit is right. You're being nosy and want the 411 on my love life."

She grins unapologetically. "You've never had a love life for me to stick my nose into before."

I shrug. "This is true."

I follow her into our tiny break room and grab a couple of plates from the dish rack while she grabs a couple of beers from the refrigerator. It has been a long time since we've bullshitted about life in general. Most of our conversations over the last two years revolve around the center and the growth we want to accomplish.

On paper, Janey owns the land and the buildings and in the beginning, she was a sole proprietor of the VKC, but that's about to change. Soon, all of us will own a piece of the company, although she will retain the majority.

That was my idea—a way to give everyone buy-in, but also allow severability should life and motivations for some of us change down the road.

Since the beginning, we have not been able to pay ourselves or our trainers a decent wage, but every guy here signed on knowing that this was an investment into the future and not just a job. Luckily, most of us have our military retirement or VA benefits to supplement our substandard paycheck. But if everything goes the way Janey and I plan—well, we won't be rich, but—we'll be comfortable enough to support our families.

Family.

That wasn't something I had to worry about until a couple of weeks ago. Now, I'm thinking about it more and more with each passing day.

"Thanks for the pizza." I fold a slice in half and shove it in my mouth to avoid having to talk.

Janey laughs and shakes her head. "Are you in love?"

I nod. "Think so."

"You think so?" She arches her brow.

"I mean, yes. It's just—" I wipe my mouth and lean back in my chair "—I never have been before."

"Never?"

"You tell me, Janey. I know I'm crazy about her and she's always on my mind and the more she opens up to me, the more I want to be her everything. Is that love?"

"Sounds like love to me."

I know better than to ask her if that's how she felt

about Chuck, her ex-husband. I'm the only one on this team that knows the full story behind her marriage and divorce from that asshole and even then, I don't think she's told me everything.

I doubt she ever will.

"What's your next step, big guy?" Janey asks while draining her bottle.

"Keep getting to know each other, maybe ask her to move in? I don't want her to feel pressured or rushed, even though I know I'll never want someone like I want her." I also drain my beer and set down the empty bottle. "If she wanted to get married tomorrow, I would."

Janey stares at me for a few minutes, her jaw slack and eyes searching for the truth behind my bold and uncharacteristic statement.

"Damn, Kemp. I'm happy for you, but part of me really thought you'd be a bachelor forever."

"I guess not. Not anymore."

Janey seems to realize she's gotten all she's going to get from me about my relationship with Mari and we spend the next, god only knows how long, shooting the shit about the investor coming in and the vendor fair and fundraiser we're hosting in two weeks.

I nuke a couple more slices of pizza while she grabs two more beers from the refrigerator. As she sets one down in front of me, she turns and cracks the other.

Instantly, it spews open as if shaken, spraying half the break room and dousing Janey in fermented hops and barley.

"Shit!" Janey slaps her palm over the top, containing

the fountain while entering herself in a wet T-shirt contest. If she'd been with any other guy besides one of us, she'd be a prime spectacle in some douchebag's fantasy.

Instead, I laugh my ass off and grab her a dish towel.

She turns around to face me, her blonde hair soaked and hanging in her face. "God dammit," she mutters, setting down the now mostly empty bottle and taking the towel from me.

"You look like a drowned long-haired Chihuahua." I duck when she throws a glare my way, considering with her, it could've easily been hands.

"I can't drive home like this. I smell like last call at a dive bar with two-week-old mop bucket water."

I jerk my thumb to the travel trailer we all sleep in when we stay the night out here. "Take a shower before you leave."

"Yeah, I think I'll do that."

"I'll clean up in here while you clean up yourself."

Janey grumbles the entire way, her voice carrying above the three dogs we have in the kennels and the white noise we leave on for them. I clean up the break room, wiping down the walls and cabinets before gathering up the used towels and throwing them in a garbage bag.

Guess she'll be taking those home with her tonight since it's her mess.

I grab my phone and note the time, realizing it's a bit later than I thought. Nearly nineteen thirty and no texts from Mari.

Damn, maybe I should be more thoughtful about giving her space to get shit accomplished. She's mentioned how getting her hair done can be an all-day appointment depending upon the style she goes for, but she doesn't do her nails or anything else, so I don't think I'm keeping her from much self-care besides bikini waxes, which I have driven her to myself.

Don't get me wrong. I like her any way I can get her, but she likes waxing most of it off—and who am I to dictate how she plates and serves me my meal?

I'm just happy to be eating.

Still, I half expected a little sassy note from her, teasing me until bedtime.

Part of me wants to call her, but I push that desire down, giving her the space she's been lacking for the last two weeks. Besides, I'll be talking to her in a few hours. I can wait.

And that is something I've been telling myself every time the desire to tell her I love her feels overwhelming.

You can wait.

Don't rush her.

It can wait.

VETERAN
K9
TEAM
REPORTING
FOR DUTY

Chapter Ten
Mari

I quickly clean my house, change my sheets and throw a load of linens in the washer, but honestly, there isn't nearly as much to do as I thought.

I've been washing my uniforms and other clothes at Kemp's house during the week. Actually, he's the one who has been doing my laundry and hanging up my ACUs with more care than I normally do.

He grabs groceries on his way home most days and cooks dinner for me most nights, pampering me in a way I've never before experienced.

It's been amazing. He's the most thoughtful man I've ever dated, but what's even better is that he never calls attention to his actions. Kemp is not a man looking for praise or credit. He genuinely wants to spend time with me.

Last Sunday he played his guitar for me, his insecurities laid bare on the floor. But his sharing it with me tore down any remaining walls I had around my heart. While

I haven't said the words out loud, I know I have completely fallen in love with him.

Cher knows and is happy for us, but she and Vale aren't pushing for couple dates just yet. She knows how I am and the pressure of displaying my feelings for another publicly is too much just yet.

Still, once I got my laundry in the washer and realized I didn't have a ton of chores to do, I swung by the grocery store and bought a smattering of hot and cold foods from the deli, deciding to surprise Kemp out at the VKC with a picnic dinner.

It seems I can't be away from him for twenty-four hours.

I guess I am in love.

Pulling into the parking lot, I'm surprised and immediately suspicious to find Janey's Dodge Charger still there with Kemp's Jeep. While he's open with me about pretty much everything, Janey is the one person he's tight-lipped about. Anytime I've asked about her ex-husband or why he and she are so close, he says the guy was an asshole and otherwise he can't really talk about it because *"it's not his story to tell."*

I've tried to keep my suspicions at bay and respect her privacy, but their secretive friendship is something that gnaws at me—especially since they work together and have fourteen years of deployments and experiences. While I know this is one hundred percent my brain and past trauma at work, it's hard to keep my feelings in check when it's dark outside and the only two people left in this secluded locale are my man and his female boss.

Shit.

I square my shoulders and take my bags of goodies to the front door to find it locked. I know he said they sleep in a trailer out back, so I round the building in the pitch black of a winter night and hear the shower turn off from outside the trailer. My heart instantly plummets into my stomach as bile rises to the back of my throat.

"Fuck, fuck, fuck." I mutter, imagining the worst while telling myself to keep an open mind and trust Kemp.

I knock on the door and Janey answers wearing a towel and nothing else. "Mari?"

At the same time, the back door to the facility opens and Kemp's large frame fills the doorway. "Mari?"

"Fuck this." I drop the groceries and run for my car, too overwhelmed to deal with the rush of visceral reaction I'm having to the situation.

Did I catch them fucking? No. But my insides twist into knots just the same.

"Mari!" I hear Kemp bark behind me at the same time the toe of my hiking boot hits the concrete sidewalk connecting the side building to the main center. Flying through the air, I land in the gravel, scraping up my palms as I do the bare minimum to protect my face. My toe instantly throbs in my boot, followed by my right knee and hands screaming in protest.

"Fuck." Kemp is kneeling next to me, rolling me onto my butt and into his arms. "Are you okay?"

"I can't do this." I shake my head as unbidden tears roll down my cheeks.

"Can't do what?" Kemp's blue eyes shine despite the darkness surrounding us. "Why the fuck did you run from me?"

"Don't you understand?" I snap. "I. Can't. Do. This."

Janey jogs up in a pair of well-worn sweats that fit her, her hair wet and hanging loose around her pretty face. At least I know they aren't his clothes—otherwise, I might lose my shit on her and I'm not sure that's a fight I would win.

"Are you okay?" she asks softly.

"I'm fine," I grumble, not looking at either of them.

"I'm sure this looks bad, Mari, but I swear to you nothing is going on," Janey says, striking right at the heart of my insecurities.

"What?" Kemp says, hooking his fingers under my chin. "You don't think—"

"I don't want to talk about it," I grit out through clenched teeth while jerking my face away from his touch.

"Oh, fuck no." Before I can stop him, Kemp hauls me up into his arms and carries me back toward the trailer.

"I'll grab the first aid kit," Janey says, running back into the building as Kemp steps over the groceries and up the three stairs into the travel trailer.

"Just let me go home," I say with half the force and even less of the enthusiasm required to be taken seriously. While my body hurts, my pride is shredded.

"Like that's going to fucking happen. If I have to tie you to this shitty plywood bed frame, I will, but make no mistake, Shorty. You are staying and talking this out with me." Kemp sets me down gently, a frown twisting his mustache as his eyes slide over me to check for injuries. There is a fresh tear in the knee of my jeans and my palms are scraped up, but it's my toe that worries me.

"Here." Janey jumps in with a first aid kit and hands it to Kemp, who keeps his eyes on me.

"Are you sure you're okay?" Janey squats down in front of me. Part of me wants to kick her away, even though I know that mounting feeling is ridiculous.

"I'm fine." I shiver, my waning adrenaline and the cold realization that I'm going to be alone for the rest of my life seeping into my bones.

"Look, Mari. Kemp and I have known each other for fourteen years and I swear, if I found him remotely attractive, something would've happened a long time ago. As it is—" her eyes slide his way when I finally meet her gaze "—physically I find him repugnant."

"Hey!" Kemp barks. "I have feelings, you know."

"Do you though?" Janey stands up and puts her hands on her hips like a sassy little sister would. "I've never seen them before."

"Get out." He unceremoniously rips my jeans to reveal the bloody scrapes on my knee. "Now."

She puts her hands up in surrender and takes a few steps backward toward the door. "If you want to talk, Mari. Grab my number."

"Out, LaVey." He points at the door but keeps his eyes on me.

I don't know why, but her willingness to connect with me makes me feel a little better.

"Good night, you two." She puts the groceries on the table and closes the door behind her, leaving me and Kemp in an awkward mess.

My man grabs the hydrogen peroxide and a handful of cotton balls. "This is going to sting."

"I'm sorry." I hiss as he dabs my cuts. "But I can't do this."

Kemp stays very still, his gaze focused on the task of fixing me up. "Janey stayed late. We ate pizza, drank a couple beers and bullshitted about the future of the center and how I've fallen in love with you."

I suck in my breath and shake my head. "Don't say that."

He brings his eyes up to meet mine. "It's true. I love you, Mari. And if you need me to share my location when we're not together or sleep on this shitty bed with me on the nights I have to be out here or call every hour on the hour to gain your trust, I'll do it."

"That's not fair. It's not right. You shouldn't have to do that because my brain is fucked up." I shake my head, tears streaming down my cheeks again. I swear, I've never cried like this in front of a man before.

Kemp kneels in front of me and cups my face, holding me as firmly as he does when his fingers are wrapped around my throat. "No, it's not right, and it's not fair, but that's what I'll fucking do until I've earned your trust. I understand no man has ever given you a reason to believe him, so let me be the first. What would convince you that you're the only woman for me?"

"Tell me again." I grip his shoulders and dig my fingertips into his muscles.

"I love you." He leans forward and rests his forehead against mine.

"I love you too."

"Is that enough?"

A desperate plea rips from my throat. "It has to be because I don't want to lose you."

"You're not. You won't. I'm never letting you go."

I straddle his lap and wrap my arms around his neck, claiming his lips like he's claimed mine so many times before. We kiss like we're each other's oxygen, our tongues tangling while our raw emotions are laid bare.

Kemp picks me up and lies down on the double mattress, stretching his big body out beside me. He stares down at me with a wry smile while using his fingers to trace along my cheekbones, my jawline and across my lips. "Couldn't stay away from me for one night, huh?"

"My pussy missed you," I smirk, trying for levity. Even though I'm embarrassed by my actions, I'm thankful Kemp is unfazed by my antics. I haven't wanted to do the work or put myself out there for a man in a long time, but he keeps showing me that he's worth it.

He trails his finger down my throat, between my breasts, and to the buttons of my jeans. "She craves my cock filling her up."

"Yes, she does."

Kemp yanks my buttons free and slides his hands inside my panties, his fingers finding my clit without issue. Slowly, torturously, he circles the little nub with the barest amount of pressure—letting me know he's here with me, but not enough to take control of my pleasure.

Not yet, anyway—although the threat, or more to the point, the promise, is there.

"No more running, Mari. I get that you have shit to work through. I also get that there will be times when the feelings in the pit of your gut will overrule all rational thought—just like they do for me. But you have to promise that you'll talk to me, fight with me, tell me to fuck those feelings out of you—whatever it takes for us to get on the same page. Okay?"

"I'll try. For you, for us, I'll try."

He narrows his eyes, applying a bit more pressure. "I'll take it—for now. Love you, Shorty."

"I love you, Michael Kemp."

VETERAN
K9
TEAM

REPORTING
FOR DUTY

Epilogue
Kemp - Six Months Later

The following weekend, Mari moved into my place and we've rented her house out ever since. It's the same thing Vale and Cher did as soon as they found out she was pregnant. In this economy, with housing prices like they are, it's a smart investment.

Of course, we're renting to two female soldiers from Fort Carson, which means whenever there is a problem or repair to do, I do not go over there unaccompanied. Although I couldn't tell you what color their eyes are, I don't need to bring that suspicion into our household or our relationship. A little thoughtfulness on my part bolsters Mari's faith in me and we're all good.

Right now we're here to turn on the sprinklers after a long winter and wet spring that is quickly turning into a dry summer.

Mari chats with the women on the front porch while I'm busy testing the three zones when both of our phones go off with this crazy ringtone Cher made us download three weeks ago.

"Holy shit!" Mari jumps up, knocking over the iced tea our renters graciously made for us. "It's time."

I pull my phone out of my pocket and sure as shit, there's a text from Vale. "It happened fast. Baby girl, seven pounds two ounces, nineteen inches long, born today at six seventeen this morning. She's healthy, beautiful, perfect and waiting for her aunt and uncle to come meet her. Mom is amazing and resting comfortably. Memorial Hospital. Room three seventeen."

I quickly turn off the water and glance up at our tenants as Mari grabs her bag. "We've got to go, but we'll come by later to finish this."

"Go!" The girls cheer as Mari and I rush to her Jeep.

"We've got to stop by the house so I can grab her presents." Mari throws her vehicle into gear. "I can't believe I'm an auntie!"

We arrive at the hospital to find Vale and Cher relaxing with a bundle wrapped in pink in Vale's arms. I have to admit, I never thought I'd see the day and the vision of him holding something so tiny stirs up feelings I've never felt.

"Hey," Vale says softly, with notably dark circles under his eyes.

Mari rushes over and gives Cher a quick hug before dropping down to kneel next to Vale.

"Oh my godddddd..." she half whispers, half coos.

He chuckles and stands up, tilting his head to the now vacant chair. "You want to hold your niece Cari?"

"Cari?" Her eyes fill up with tears as she takes a seat and opens her arms.

Cher nods. "Yeah, a merging of our names. Friends for life, right?"

"Right." Mari glances up at me and I swear it's a donkey kick to my gut. Wordlessly, our future unfolds in front of us and I know kids are on the horizon.

"How are you holding up?" I ask Vale, who looks like he's about to fall over.

"Good. Tired, but good." He slips his hand into Cher's and brings it up to his mouth. "Cher went into labor around midnight. We got here an hour later and Cari came out a few hours after that."

"Wow."

"Yeah. I've called our parents and they are on their way. Our house is going to be overrun with grandparents soon."

"You want us to take Sookie and Strijker for a couple of days to give you some room?"

"That would be good. Actually, can you stop by on your way home and give them a break?"

"Absolutely, man. Consider it done."

I return my gaze to Mari, who looks natural holding a newborn infant in her arms. I knew I was going to marry her the day I asked her to move in, but I wasn't sure about kids. Now that I've seen her holding a baby, I can't imagine not having a child with her.

Kneeling beside her, I peek in on the bundle with her cute button nose and then look at my woman's face glowing with pure love and adoration. "You look good holding a baby, Shorty."

She grins. "Do I?"

"Yeah, I like it."

"We'd make a pretty baby," she whispers while tracing Cari's chubby cheeks with her finger.

"As soon as you're ready." I lean forward and press a kiss to her neck.

Mari's breath catches. "Are you serious?"

"I'll put a ring on your finger tomorrow and a baby in your belly tomorrow night if you want me to. Just say the word."

She scrunches up her nose. "I hope that wasn't your proposal."

Chuckling, I shake my head. "No, but that doesn't make my words any less true."

"It would be nice—if we do have kids—that they are around Vale and Cher's kids' ages. You know, so they can grow up together and stuff."

I glance down at the little girl with a mess of bright red on her tiny little head. "Then we better get your birth control removed while I plan the perfect proposal."

Little does Mari know, but I bought her ring months ago and already planned on proposing to her on our one-year anniversary celebration up at Estes Park. That's still two months away, and it's been torture waiting to pop the question while keeping our vacation plans a secret.

After nearly an hour of hanging out, Mari and I make our way home to let Cher and Vale get some rest. We swing by their house and pick up Sookie and Strijker, taking them home with us. Once I have the dogs settled, I walk into the bedroom to find Mari sitting in the middle of our bed playing with a bundle of purple cotton rope. "What's going on?"

"Do you really want to have a baby?"

I sit on the edge of the bed and grab one end of the rope. "I want a life with you, however that looks. As long as we're together, that's all that matters."

"But do you want kids?" She lets go of the rope when I give a gentle tug and immediately presents me with her forearms to play with.

"It's like you said—" I quickly find the bit of the rope and make a hitch crossing the strands up her arms in a pretty pattern "—we'd make a pretty baby, especially if they look like you."

"With your eyes." She grins. "But not your beard because that would make the baby look ridiculous."

I yank the binds and pull her forward so her elbows hit the mattress and her ass comes up in the air. "You are begging to be spanked."

"Mmmm. And fucked like a good little whore."

"My whore." I hold her face in my hand and kiss her deeply, all the love I never knew I could feel for another pouring out of me.

"Fuck me good, Ragnar. And later we'll practice making a baby later when you make love to me."

VETERAN
K9
TEAM
REPORTING
FOR DUTY

Second Epilogue
Mari - Six years later

"How is it possible that today is Mallory's first day of Kindergarten?" I place the crafty sign I made for her first day pictures inside the door before grabbing her pink and purple unicorn backpack with matching lunchbox. Where Cher and I were tomboys most of our lives, our daughters—Mallory, Cari, and Jessie—are all princesses. Well, maybe not Cari, who went as a Wookie ballerina last Halloween. She's got a good sense of balance between her feminine and masculine energies.

Kemp smiles down at our daughter and shrugs as tears well up in his eyes. "Hell if I know."

I slip my hand in his and squeeze before running back inside to grab my purse. Before I know it, we're leaving a calm and collected Mallory at school with her friend Johnnie, and walking back to the parking lot with Cher and Vale.

Cher smiles at me. "You going to be okay, Momma Bear?"

"Yeah. I think so." I waggle my fingers at Jessie who Vale is strapping into his car seat.

"Did you take my advice?" Cher whispers conspiratorially to me.

"Yep. Kemp and I both took the day off."

"Good. Have fun." She grins and gives me a quick hug. "If you get tied up and need us to grab Mallory at the end of the day, let me know."

I reach out to smack her arm, but she's already dancing away from me, her lyrical laughter causing me to grin and shake my head.

I never should have told her about the Shibari. "Wench."

"You love me."

"Yeah, I do."

Vale's lips twitch, but he says nothing as he gives me a chin tilt and closes Jessie and then Cher's car doors. He fist bumps Kemp and waves over his head as he rounds the front of their giant Suburban. "See you guys later."

Kemp slides his hand onto the small of my back, his fingers gripping the back of my pants in a commanding hold. "Ready to go home, Shorty?"

He only calls me Shorty when it's the two of us and sex is on the horizon. At this point it's foreplay, and has an almost Pavlovian effect on me—sending tingles through my body to culminate in my pussy.

I grin. "More than ready."

We drive home in contemplative silence. As Kemp pulls into our driveway and puts our SUV in park before he slides his big palm onto my thigh and squeezes.

"Remember that purple sundress you wore to the picnic last month?"

"Yeah?"

"Go inside, put on that dress with nothing underneath, and meet me downstairs in ten minutes. Be on your knees when I get there."

I narrow my eyes—my natural inclination to argue—and press my lips together when he raises his brow. "Okay."

Over the years I've learned that sometimes a little resistance makes the sex even hotter, but the more I resist, the harder Kemp has to push, which is emotionally taxing on him sometimes. We're more in tune now than ever before, and I suspect that will only get better over time. Today has been emotional day for both of us with our baby taking her first big girl steps into the world, and I know Kemp's been just as nervous as I've been.

Not just nervous, but sad and happy, excited and overwhelmed.

Really, it's a lot of fucking emotion for something as simple as the first day of school—and today, Kemp needs me compliant. He'll get me out of my head while I get him out of his, and we'll be mentally and physically sated by the time we have to pick up Mallory this afternoon.

I quickly rinse off in the shower, throw my hair up in a ponytail, and slip on the sundress before tiptoeing downstairs to our basement / playroom. Kemp is outside with Krieger, who at nine years old, is an old man and requires special food with his medication. I know watching him deteriorate weighs on Kemp, another emotional burden my man shoulders without complaint.

The backdoor opens and closes, and Kemp's boots thud on the hardwood in the kitchen above me as he kicks them off. My man clears his throat before his feet hit the stairs, and I drop to my knees in front of the weight bench that happens to strategically have a giant eye-bolt screwed into the joist above it.

He comes around the corner, his gaze landing on me and a pleased smile on his face. "Fuck me, you are the most beautiful thing I've ever seen. Do I tell you that often enough, Shorty?"

I nod. "Yes. You take good care of me, Ragnar."

He pulls something out of his pocket and sits on the weight bench next to me. "I got you something."

"An early anniversary present?" Our anniversary is two months away. Six years together, but it feels like I met him yesterday. I still remember the butterflies in my tummy the first time we met at the Last Stand.

He shakes his head and opens the box to reveal a gold chain with a solid gold bar pendant hanging from it. "This is your first day of school present."

Inspecting the engraving, I see my name, Mallory, and Kemp on three of the sides, but the engraving on the backside is too small for my eyes to make out. "What's it say?"

Grinning, Kemp reaches around my neck and fastens the clasp, positioning the pendant between my breasts on the long chain. "Kemp's good little whore."

"That I am." I melt when he leans forward and

claims my lips in a sweet kiss that quickly turns fevered. "From now until we're too old to fuck."

"Even when we're too old, Shorty. You will always be mine."

Coming next: Barron and Betty in Mine to Possess

Most of my books take place in Spring City, Colorado and feature cameo appearances from characters in past / present / and sometimes future books from all of my series. Check out my website for a cross-over / series map.

Also by Kameron Claire

Want more **Witty** Tongues, **Wicked** Needs, & **Wild** Deeds?

Hollywood Lights (Pre-Order)

* Billionaire Romance *

Show Time (Securing Selyne)

Money Shot

Three Shot

Martini Shot

Long Shot

Veteran K9 Team

** Military Romance **

Mine to Cherish

Mine to Crave

Mine to Possess

Mine to Adore

Mine to Covet

Mine to Worship

Mine to Protect

Mine to Treasure

Hot Nights with the Boss

** Forbidden Office / Age-Gap Romances **

Dating the Boss

Flirting with the Boss

Teasing the Boss

Tempting the Boss

Rangers Football

** Sports Romance **

Play Action Fake

Quarterback Sneak

Personal Foul

Two-Point Conversion

Red Zone

Man to Man Coverage

Short Story Collections and Bundles

Animal Attraction 4-Story Collection

Vegas Nights 4-Story Collection

Last Stand Saloon 4-Story Collection

Instalove Bundle

Grayson Enterprises Series

Bedding the Boss

Enticing the Ex

Tempting the Teacher

Wedding the Widow

About the Author

 USA Today Bestselling Author Kameron Claire writes stories with witty tongues, wicked needs, and wild deeds. Her books emphasize strong female leads and the protective alpha males who know how to love and support kick-ass, take-charge women. Many of her books contain military veterans, boss babes, gentle but dominant men, and goofy K9 hijinks.

Find her everywhere via linktr.ee/kameronclaire
Signed Paperbacks and discounted eBook bundles are available exclusively on her store
Subscribe to the Witty, Wicked & Wild community and read all her books online for as little as $5 a month.